White Ghost Summer

White Ghost Summer

by Shirley Rousseau Murphy

ILLUSTRATED BY BARBARA McGEE

THE VIKING PRESS/New York

Viking Seafarer edition
Issued in 1969 by The Viking Press, Inc.
625 Madison Avenue, New York, N.Y. 10022
Distributed in Canada by
The Macmillan Company of Canada Limited
Library of Congress catalog card number: AC 67-10405
Fic 1. Horses—Stories
2. Mystery stories
SBN 670–05020–2
2   3   4   5   6   76   75   74   73   72

Printed in U.S.A.

For my husband, my mother,
and for Alice M. Turner.

Chapter 1

Look at that old house, gray and tired, pressed on both sides by other houses, choked with telephone wires and blinded by smudged windows. Garbage cans sit on the curb, and two small girls in faded dresses play with shabby dolls on the concrete steps.

It is a tall house with many windows, and with six apartments inside.

In that window near the top which juts out like a half-tower, where the pale curtains are, sits another girl. She is not playing with dolls. She is only sitting, watching the little girls below and thinking how dull it must be, playing with those grimy dolls on that dusty stoop. The street is hot and treeless, the buildings crowding roof to roof.

This girl wants a tree to climb, grass to roll in. She wants a leafy, breezy sky. There are no trees, no grass. The sky is muddy and hot.

A gray truck comes clanging into the street and stops before the garbage cans. The garbage men look at the little girls on the steps in an unfriendly way, as though it is too hot to be pleasant.

The girl in the window has a piece of bread in her hand, and she watches the roof across the way. Soon a whirling and flapping comes through the sky and a ragged, fusty old pigeon lands on the window sill beside her. "At least this city has pigeons," she has said so many times. "At least it has something alive."

He coos at her knowingly and she breaks off bits of bread and hands them to him. He is very tame, really nervy.

She is a small, lean child. She has curly red hair, cut short, and there is a bang across her forehead and a flock of freckles across her nose. Her eyes are big and dark.

She runs out of bread finally, and the pigeon flaps and coos impatiently. She disappears from the window and re-appears several minutes later with more. The pigeon fusses and struts while she is gone.

"Don't be so cross," she tells him. "You can fly away. I can't."

The pigeon coos.

"You can go to the seashore," she says, "and bathe in the water and scratch in the sand, and you can go where there is grass and catch caterpillars. Nobody makes you stay in the city, eating stale old bread from a dirty window sill.

"Look at you, you have lice." The pigeon is scratching and fluffing his feathers and pecking under his wing. "I bet you wouldn't in the country." This isn't true and she knows it, but it makes her feel better.

"You're just a dirty, scraggly pigeon with soot on his tail," she tells him. "You don't even have sense enough to get out of the city in the summertime." Just then the door slams open behind her. The pigeon flutters from the sill and flaps back across the street.

The girl's sister stands in the doorway, hot and panting. She has a large satchel of books weighting her down on one side, and a dirty gym suit under the other arm. Even though it is summer in the city, it is only the next to last week of school.

Melani hangs her head down off the window seat, looking at her older sister upside down. Zee Zee puts her books on a chair and throws the gym suit in a laundry basket by the closet door. Her brown hair is longer and straighter than Mel's, ending in an undecided curve at the base of her neck. She starts to pull off her jumper and get into a pair of shorts. She drops her hot, sweaty clothes into the basket after the gym suit.

"It's not the heat so much, it's the dry smelliness of it," says Zee Zee.

"Yes," says Mel, "and nowhere to go."

"That's what I mean," says Zee Zee. Her name is Cecelia, but she has always been Zee Zee. "No place to get away from it." She does not mind the city as much as Mel does, but she minds it enough, certainly.

"Maybe Mother will find a house this time," says Mel, "with trees."

"Yes," says Zee Zee, "and six bedrooms."

"Mmmm," says Mel.

The pigeon comes back to the window and starts cooing for more bread.

The girls hear their younger brother come slamming through the front door below. Dinner will be soon. Linda and Deb will be laying the table. Mel and Zee Zee start down to help.

Just as they are at the top of the stairs they hear another slam. This will be Mother. They pause, waiting to hear shoes and purse dropped tiredly. There is no other sound from below. They peep over the railing, then run helter-skelter down the stairs.

Mother is standing in the hall waiting for them. She doesn't say a word, but she is smiling. The two older girls come from the kitchen, wiping their hands. Jeffy, the gray, shaggy sheep dog, follows them, and the black-and-white cat comes out from under the stairs.

"You've found it," shout Mel and Zee Zee together. "You've found a house."

"Yes," says Mother, "I've found it. You'll have a long bus ride to school the next two weeks."

"You mean we can move right away?" they all shout at once. "But what's it like?"

"Where is it?"

"When can we see it?"

"How do you know we'll like it?"

"You'll like it," says Mother. "You'll like it all right."

"Does it have trees?" asks Zee Zee.

"And grass?" asks Mel.

"Where is it?" They are all begging.

"You'll see," says Mother. "After dinner you'll see."

"Will Aunt Vivian like it?" asks Mel.

"No," says Mother, "she won't."

They all look delighted. If Aunt Vivian won't like it, they know they will.

"She doesn't have to live in it," says Spence.

"No," says Linda, "she doesn't."

Chapter 2

From the windows of the house one could see green things and fogs rising and winds stirring the clouds overhead. There was blue sea, and there were tall dark trees towering and golden-leafed trees blowing. There was grass and birds. There was sunlight.

No one had imagined that a city house could be like this, but there it was, where the city stopped at the edge of the Pacific and the city park came to meet the seashore.

It stood on a corner, other houses on two sides of it, but in front of it only a street, then a strip of sand, and then the sea. To the left as you faced the sea was the park, thickly treed, rich with breezes.

From everywhere in the house you could hear the sea crashing on the beach and hear the gulls call as they wheeled after picnickers' leavings.

"You could have a smaller house," said Aunt Vivian,

sipping tea. "A newer one. Closer to town, and neater. The girls could share a room; girls should share a room. And you should get a regular job, Susan. It's not steady, working at home."

"But the girls do not want to share a room," said Mother. "We each want our own room, and space to move in."

Zee Zee set the silver tray of teacakes on the coffee table. Mel and Deb and Linda sat stiffly among the chattering ladies. Spencer squirmed. His collar was choking him, and his new shoes squeezing.

"But such a monstrous, unkempt old house," Aunt Vivian was saying. "It is much too large and out of date. Whatever made you buy it, Susan?" She sat in the best yellow chair, next to the window which looked on the park, and she fingered her embroidered napkin peevishly.

The other ladies clicked their tongues and took more teacakes. It was all terribly proper. Mother was quiet and polite—angry, Zee Zee knew.

If she gets angry enough, she will shout, thought Mel deliciously.

The ladies had already been conducted over the whole house, upstairs and down, stepping around the boxes and crates that still stood in the great old rooms. Last of all, Mother had shown them the attic.

None of them could climb the ladder, but all had stood staring up at the little patch of rafters they could see, looking amazed when told that Zee Zee slept there.

"We all chose our own rooms," said Mother.

One more pouring out of tea, one more passing of cakes, and finally they were gone.

"Ah," said Mother.

"Ah," they all said.

It was not a monstrous old house. It was big and old, but it was lovely and strange, with odd juttings and turnings and unexpected windows and hidden nooks. It had a cellar, and even an apartment built under the house.

Aunt Kelly would have the apartment. "Oh, she's not like Aunt Vivian, is she?" they all cried.

"No," said Mother, "she's not."

Aunt Vivian would have said, "No, she is certainly not. I was your *father's* sister."

"Is Aunt Kelly like you, Mother?" asked Zee Zee.

"Perhaps a little," said Mother. "Wait and see."

"Is she redheaded too?" asked Mel.

"Yes," said Mother, "but turning gray."

"Oh," said Mel, disappointed, "she's old."

"You won't think so," said Mother.

Melani's room faced the park. Her windows showed her sky and trees and birds, grass to roll in, trees to climb. Mother's room was next to it on one side, Spencer's on the other.

Across the hall was Mother's studio. Its tall windows, side by side, lined two walls, floor to ceiling, flooding the room with pearly light even on the foggiest days. The ladies had seemed puzzled at the idea of a studio in a house, at the great drafting table, the huge paper-cutter, and at the smells of paint and ink and board, of chalk and lacquer and turpentine. "Unfeminine," said one. The girls had giggled in spite of themselves.

Each person's room was just right. Spencer's had a balcony where he could put his snakes to bask in the sun. Spencer was a rough, tough little boy, redheaded like Mel. He didn't care for anything in the whole world as much as he cared for his snakes. It's funny, thought Zee Zee, how different we all are. How could I ever be like Spencer, or refined and quiet like Deb? Though of course she is older. Debra's dark hair was always neat, her tall figure graceful. She had clever hands that could help Mother and earn professional pay for it.

Zee Zee's hands liked to make things, too, but somehow her mind always went faster than her fingers. "Not mine," said Deb. "I like to do things slowly."

"I don't need to be neat to build cages," said Spence.

"I would rather do something else," said Mel. "I don't like to be still." She was eleven, Spence nine. Zee Zee was thirteen, Debra and Linda, seventeen.

Linda, of course, was not related. She was adopted. Her surname had been made the same as theirs—Heath. Her hair was black, like Deb's, her eyes dark and laughing. "You are not going to have Debra sleeping right next to that Mexican girl's room," said Aunt Vivian.

"They are the same age," Mother said. "And remember, Vivian, their fathers were soldiers together; they died in the same battle."

"But," Aunt Vivian said, "should they be downstairs, alone like that?"

"Why not?" said Mother. "Spence and Mel are the troublemakers; their rooms are best near mine. Zee Zee is fine in the attic."

"Hmph," said Aunt Vivian.

Chapter 3

Zee Zee's walls had been painted that morning. Deb had helped her, though there was not much to paint. The rafters of the high peaked ceiling came down to meet the floor on two sides of the room, making triangular walls at each end, newly white. In one of these an immense window rose to the rafters. It's like the inside of the Ark, thought Zee Zee. The sun slanted through the window in the late afternoon, making an orange path over the sea and turning the warm wood of the ceiling to a golden sculpture overhead. It made the spider webs between the rafters dance like fairy ladders, and the little Persian rug on the floor gleam richly.

Zee Zee's books were still piled helter-skelter around the room, and she began to fill the low shelves with them.

At the side of the room, where the ceiling met the floor, was Zee Zee's low bed, snug under the rafters, and next to it, her old chest, newly painted red—"Chinese red," Deb said—and with new brass handles. Her desk stood under the great window facing the sea.

In the far corner there were three steps leading up, and at the top was another little attic room almost like a stage. At the back of this a low door led into still another attic. Zee Zee had discovered it after they had moved in, on the first morning that she had awakened there, listening to the sea through her open window and gazing about her happily.

There had been an old piece of wallboard nailed crookedly at the back of the little room, and as she began to pull the nails to take it down the discovery of a door made her run calling to tell Mother.

"Open it," said Mother, still in curlers and pajamas. Zee Zee did. It led into a room as immense as Mother's studio. The ceiling sloped as in the smaller attic room, but it was higher, with crossbeams beneath the rafters and the peak towering above them. The room was lined with boxes and trunks, and they began—Mother with no coffee at all, sleep still in their eyes—to explore what was there.

Finally Mother said, "No, I must have some coffee. Come on," and they made a tray with coffee and cocoa and toast and jam. They were so quiet that Linda and Deb did not even stir.

There were scraps of everything in the world in those boxes. The dust rose up around them a little as they pried and rummaged. There were trunks full of snips and pieces of cloth: some silk, some lace, some cotton, some brocaded and very rich.

There were trunks filled with bits of hardwoods, brown

and golden. There were little sheets of clear plastic, and tiny jars of paint. There were trunks of pale balsa wood in different thicknesses and sizes, and there were scraps of leather and wool, bits of colored glass and mosaic tile.

"It looks," said Mother, "like the leftover stock from a hobby shop. All but the cloth. Those are sewing scraps."

In the corner of the attic was an old table as big as Zee Zee's bed.

There was a bare light bulb hanging from the center of the ceiling. "You can put a shade over that," said Mother.

"Then it's to be my room, too," said Zee Zee.

"Yes," said Mother, "it is."

From the other side of the house, away from Zee Zee's attic, one could see the park across the way. From Mother's room, from Melani's, and Spencer's, you could look out on the old twisted cypress trees which knelt before the wind, and then on to the park proper, or the beginning of it, for it was no small city park; it went on for miles in a wide, green strip of hills and valleys, of flowering trees and bridle paths and heavy, wild thickets. It was a place to lie on your back and watch the sky and smell the breezes and wander in until you were lost; a place for Mel —oh, wonderful agony—to see horses in. Horses and ponies, in ones and twos and in whole classes, went along the bridle paths all day, walking, cantering, trotting out nice and open, and Mel, when she was not right there watching, could see them all from her window. Even sitting up in bed she could see, for she had her bed by the window, and her desk against it, too. It made the room lopsided, but no one cared.

The park was often foggy and mysterious in the mornings. The first morning that Mel saw the horses on the bridle path it was like this, so that they floated like fairy horses, their ears pricking the mists.

"I saw them, I saw them, there are horses in the park," she screamed at Linda, who was buttering toast.

"You knew there were," said Linda, grinning. "Were they beautiful?"

"I know I did, but now I've seen them. Oh, yes, they were. There were three. Three beautiful, magic horses."

"Who was riding them? Witches?" asked Spencer. He had too much jam on his toast and it was running down his hand.

Mel stuck out her tongue.

Debra came in and zipped Linda's dress, then turned around for her own. Linda wiped her hands first, making her wait. "Toast crumbs down your back?" she asked as Deb sighed impatiently.

"There were horses this morning, Deb," Mel said again, sighing, wishing Spencer would spill jam on his cords and have to change.

"Yes," said Deb, "I heard. What time were you out?"

"About five, I guess. I didn't look."

"Five-fifteen," said Linda. "She took two slices of chicken and a radish with her."

"Ah," said Deb, "you won't need breakfast then."

"I will," said Mel. "Fog makes me hungry."

"We'll be late for school," said Deb, stirring eggs.

"Not on the last day," said Linda.

And they were not.

Chapter 4

Mel could never stay in bed after the first pale daylight touched her window, and for this reason as much as anything, old Jeff chose her bed to sleep on. The two of them made fine footprints in the early morning dew, dog and human, side by side.

Sometimes it was so foggy that they could scarcely see ahead of them. They would cross the street carefully, Jeffy nudging close and sniffing the brown paper bag in Mel's hand, and when on the other side wade deliciously in the cold dew until they had lost themselves from the world, forever it seemed.

Then they would share the contents of the bag; whatever one ate, so did the other. Salad, pickles, cold spaghetti.

Breakfast over, they would continue to wander, Mel

thoroughly lost, Jeffy wise but pretending, until the mists finally rose or hunger drove them home again.

One morning, sitting on a little hill, huddled together to keep warm, wishing there were more cookies (there had been only five), and gazing out over the sea of fog as it settled into the valley, Mel and Jeffy saw the ghost. They were the first to see it.

The whole park was like a thick white sea, dotted here and there with the tops of hills, like little islands, and

pierced weirdly by the tops of the tallest trees. The sky was washed with thin, blowing mists.

Dreamily, sleepily (unwashed and unbrushed), Mel leaned on Jeffy's shoulder and began to imagine. A wild, handsome stallion lives on these islands, she pretended. He is grazing there, behind those trees. Soon he will come out and stand staring at me. He has never seen people before, so he is not afraid. He will come toward me. I will be very still. I will put out my hand, gently, like this. . . .

The mists were changing, growing thinner in spots. Something was moving within them.

And then above the thick fog appeared a ghostly, pale horse. The mists seemed to move right through him. He was silvery white, with a silver-gray mane and tail caught in the mists. He was looking directly at Mel, ears forward. He seemed to float before her. Then he reared, wheeled slowly, and was gone.

The park was as quiet as a tomb. Jeffy's ears pricked forward. His tail flopped once when Mel whispered to him, but he continued to stare.

Panda, the cat, was not as early a riser as were Jeffy and Mel. He liked to lie in bed a little later and have Zee Zee rub his stomach.

"He is getting old," said Mother.

"No, he's not," said Zee Zee. "Just dignified."

This morning he was stretching with delight, purring loudly, flicking his tail slightly, when suddenly he stiffened, flipped over on his feet, and growled softly at the door. Then he recognized Mel's whisper and settled down again.

"Zee Zee! Zee Zee, wake up!" whispered Mel, climbing the ladder, Jeffy standing, wet-footed, below, whining softly. She went back down and set a chair for him so that he could come, too; then she climbed up once more and piled onto Zee Zee's bed, fog-wet and muddy.

"I am awake," said Zee Zee. "What's the matter? You look . . ."

"I saw a ghost," said Mel.

"In the house?" asked Zee Zee, her eyes narrowing. "You were asleep, probably."

"No, in the park," said Mel, and she told her.

"Are you sure," asked Zee Zee, "it wasn't just the fog?"

"I think I'm sure," said Mel. "I think I am."

"Let's go and see," whispered Zee Zee, climbing into shorts and a shirt.

But the fog was blowing away, and though they waited until the park was clear and sunny and they were hungry, they did not see a thing except two squirrels and a rabbit.

"Are you sure you saw something?" asked Zee Zee.

"I think I am," said Mel again. "Maybe it wants only me to see it," she whispered. "Maybe it will come back." Since it was a horse ghost, she was not afraid of it. "I will see it again, I know I will."

"I won't tell anyone," said Zee Zee.

Mel squeezed her hand.

Chapter 5

If it had not been for Panda, Zee Zee might have been frightened at night in her small attic room, with the great room standing behind it. But with Panda there it was all right. He wanted the door to the big attic left open, and would pester Zee Zee if she forgot. Sometimes she could hear him in the middle of the night playing in the boxes and trunks. Are there mice there? she wondered.

"What will you do with all this?" asked Deb, fingering the contents of the boxes.

"I will make something," said Zee Zee. She had known this long ago, the minute she saw it. "I haven't decided what."

"A cuckoo's nest," said Spence.

"May I help?" asked Mel.

"Maybe," said Zee Zee. "When I decide."

The balsa wood would be easy to cut and glue, the fabric and paints were bright and beckoning. The big table waited, bare and sturdy; and the light from the tall window and the warm, still attic air, smelling of wood, were inviting. Shut away at the top of the house, very still and private, something waited to be built. But Zee Zee did not yet know what.

Perhaps a picture made of wood, she thought, or a tapestry of cloth and yarn. Perhaps a procession of wooden animals, decorated with pieces of bright cloth and paint. Perhaps a wooden zoo, but she wouldn't like her animals in cages. Perhaps a flock of brightly decorated birds in flight, hanging from the ceiling. Perhaps. Perhaps; but she did not know. Not yet.

"There is a bay horse and two chestnuts that go out in the morning. Ladies ride them," said Mel. "Snooty. They wear jodhpurs and boots and derbies. One even wears a stock."

"It is cold in the morning," said Mother.

"Yes," said Mel. "The horses snort and sometimes even buck a little."

"I'll bet they'd buck," said Spence, "if I turned my snakes loose under them."

"You'd better not," said Mel.

Though the park was mysterious and foggy in the mornings, Zee Zee liked it best when the mists had lifted and the sun was beginning to lay warm hands on the paths and hills. Often she and Mel would take a jelly sandwich each, and an apple, and lie on their stomachs in the velvety grass,

watching Jeffy roam, illegally unleashed, and count the clouds and listen for hoofbeats on the path.

"I haven't seen him anymore," said Mel, speaking of the ghost, "but I will." Zee Zee knew she went every morning to wait for him.

"I wish we could swim," said Zee Zee, thinking of the ocean.

"It's too cold," said Mel. "And dangerous, Mother said." Their strip of ocean was posted. No one swam in it.

"We could wade," said Zee Zee.

"What good is that?" said Mel.

Three horses were coming sedately down the path, their riders neat and prim. "Don't they ever canter?" asked Zee Zee.

"Oh, yes," said Mel. "Farther down, where the trail is

straight. Sometimes over that winding path on the hill, if they are good riders. What will you make in the attic?"

"I don't know yet," said Zee Zee. They were used to this kind of answer; Mother gave it often.

"What kind of pictures will you make for the book?" Mel would ask.

"I don't know yet," Mother would say. "I must think on it some more."

But Deb always seemed to know what Mother would do. "I thought you would do that," she would say. Perhaps it was because she worked so much with Mother that she knew.

Or, "What will you do for this job?" Spence would ask, and then they would all be off with suggestions, until Mother cried a stop.

"Too much, too much," she would say. "I must sleep on it some more."

That was how it was about the attic. Something wonderful was to be built there. The colors and textures of the scraps fascinated Zee Zee's hands and eyes, and she would spend hour upon hour arranging them this way and that, but what she would make she did not know. She must sleep on it.

And then for days she would forget it all together and wander the park with Mel, ankle-deep in the summer grass, the sky very blue above them.

"There is a squirrel in that tree," Mel would say, and put her hand into the sack for nuts. She would cluck, and down it would come, bold as brass, shivering toward them, faking, skittery, then grabbing delicately.

"There are real antelope in a place I know," said Mel, and sure enough, there was a fenced pasture where they grazed, brown-and-white and lovely. "They belong to the zoo," said Mel, and they did.

Spencer belonged to the zoo, too. Or at least he belonged to the snake house, body and soul. He knew the keepers, and he knew the snakes by name. "Mr. Roberts let me feed Harold today," he would say, and everyone was duly pleased.

Sometimes Mel and Zee Zee went with him, but snakes didn't interest them, and they always had to collect him by the glass cages when it was time to go. "It's a lucky thing for you the zoo is free," said Mother.

"The cats are beautiful," said Zee Zee. There was a marvelous pair of snow leopards, and a young ocelot who flirted with the children, running the length of her cage and chasing her tail like a kitten.

Other days it was quite enough to lie on a little hill in the park and watch the clouds and dream about what would be built in the attic.

Melani dreamed about other things.

"If they were not so grand," said Mel, "I would visit the stables." It took quite a magnificent grandness to cow Mel, but the stables were impressive, and the riders and trainers very business-like. "They stable hunters there," said Mel, "and polo ponies. I've seen them practice. If I had a horse, I wonder if they would let me keep him there. If I could pay, of course. A plain saddle horse, I mean."

"But there are saddle horses there, we've seen them," said Zee Zee.

"Yes, but their clothes," said Mel.

Zee Zee knew what she meant.

"But it would be lovely," said Mel. "Lovely." And she watched the horses on the trail with her brown eyes big and round with longing. She sniffed the lovely horse smell, and her longing to ride was so real that Zee Zee could almost touch it.

"Couldn't we afford lessons?" Zee Zee asked Mother.

"Yes, we can afford it," said Mother. "There may be no new clothes for school, but does anyone really care?" No one did. They were growing and the girls would change around. The older girls would get something of Mother's and Mother would do without.

"I work at home," said Mother. "I don't need much."

"Her birthday is Thursday," said Mother. "How do you wrap a package of lessons?" Zee Zee hugged Mother hard. "And what about you, Zee, don't you want riding lessons too?"

"I don't know," said Zee Zee. "Not like Melani. I have something else to do. It would be nice, but not like Melani." She knew they couldn't both. "Next time," said Zee Zee.

Chapter 6

They were wrapped in a little box, a small pink ticket for every lesson, and that in a bigger box, and that in a bigger. "Every day?" Mel was breathless. "Every single day, all summer?"

"It's the best way to learn," said Mother.

"Oh," said Mel. "Oh. Oh."

"She has already read everything there is to know about riding. She will learn very fast," said Linda.

And she had. She knew it all by heart. "I need to see how it feels," said Mel. Long ago she had found a sawhorse and padded its sides and given it rope stirrups and a broom head. She held the four reins properly. She held her heels down and kept her knees in and knew all the parts of the saddle and bridle and of a horse. She knew that you never tie a horse by the reins, and that hoofs must be examined and cleaned, and that a horse must be moved a little after the girth is tightened. She knew how the bit should fit and how tight the throatlatch should be. She knew about foundering, and about not watering a horse when he is hot. She knew about the Aids, and practiced them.

"But I don't know how it feels," said Mel. She could only imagine. The sawhorse did not move about. It did not even smell like a horse.

But now--now there was to be a real horse.

"But what about clothes?" said Mel. She had tears brimming in her eyes when she thought of it.

"I asked Mr. Blake," said Mother. "He said it wasn't necessary, that very few of the beginners had proper clothes."

Mel didn't like the sound of "beginners." Silly little girls, she thought. And some of them turned out to be just that.

"He said you could advance at your own speed," said Mother.

"Well, I will," said Mel, planning it all.

She dreamed of trotting, and woke in a sweat, wondering if she could post. She dreamed of going over a hurdle and woke whispering something about reaching for ears. She kicked and floundered and made Jeff growl softly and move to the floor, and she woke tired and cross and anxious.

But when she got to her lesson she was calm, though an hour early. She stood quietly where she was told, out of the way, and watched the class before hers. They were all big children, and they were playing tag. As the horses left the ring she turned to a little girl who had come up beside her (Wearing a ruffled blouse, thought Mel. How stupid!) and said, "Playing tag is very good; it teaches you a good seat, and makes good hands. How are your hands?" The little girl looked at Mel and fled to her mother.

"She is getting insufferable," said Debra that night.

"She will get over it," said Mother.

"I will ride that little bay gelding," Mel said to Mr. Blake.

"You will ride that gray mare," said Mr. Blake. "Her name is Patsy."

"I will ride bareback," said Mel. "It makes good hands."

"You will ride English like the rest," said Mr. Blake. "Patsy will teach you to have good hands." And he was right, she did.

Patsy did not like to have her mouth pulled. She could teach a child very quickly about good hands.

But Mel did not pull Patsy's mouth. She held the reins in both hands as she was told, lightly and with care, and she obeyed promptly. If she began to lose her balance the little mare would stop and wait for her to get reseated, and soon they were friends, Patsy always patient and Mel always gentle.

"She is making good progress," said Mr. Blake to Mother the next week. "I will put her in a different class soon. She can ride that bay gelding, Buttons. We need Patsy for the little ones, and Mel needs more of a challenge."

"A challenge?" asked Mother.

"Buttons will try some tricks with her," said Mr. Blake. "He will teach her a thing or two that Patsy is too much of a lady to teach her." Mother looked alarmed, but Mr. Blake only laughed. "He will try to rub her off under trees and against low bushes," he said. "He is very sly, but safe. And he has another trick, an original one." Mr. Blake winked, and he whispered in Mother's ear, for Mel was riding toward them.

"What were you laughing about?" asked Mel later.

"Oh, a little joke," said Mother.

"But what?" asked Mel.

"A little private joke," said Mother.

Mel laughed about it later—much later, after she had finished being mad, and after she had seen Buttons pull the same trick on another child.

"He was in the circus," explained Mel, telling Linda. "He was really a circus horse, and do you know what he learned to do? But he only did it once with me, only once," she bragged. "He sat down in the middle of the trail, just like a dog! He sat down, and I slid off right in front of the whole class." Mel's face turned quite pink.

"Yes," said Mother, after Buttons had scraped Mel under a low branch and scratched her forehead, "he is a challenge."

"He won't do that again, either," said Mel.

"They are well-matched," said Mr. Blake. "It is a contest of wits. She is learning something, and though I won't tell her, she is good for that pony. He has met his match."

Mel learned to watch what she was about when mounting, lest she be nipped in the seat or have her foot kicked smartly from the stirrup. She also learned not to hold the little gelding on a long rope, for instead of pulling away as another horse might, he would turn tail and run off so that she had no leverage with which to hold him. "He's a smart one," Mr. Blake said, laughing. He seemed to be getting as much fun out of the contest as Mel and Buttons were.

Every defeat was maddening, every victory a triumph, and in between Mr. Blake sometimes saw Mel hugging the little gelding tightly in the darkness of his stall. Though Buttons's ears were back, he seemed to be grinning.

"She must ride other horses, too," said Mr. Blake, and he put her on a rangy half-Thoroughbred mare that frightened her, and that she did not like at all. "You must," said Mr. Blake. She did as she was told, and soon she was as comfortable on Lucy as she was on the little bay gelding. But always Mel came back to Buttons; she resented the time away from him, and the other horses seemed dull.

Soon Mel was riding all of the rent horses. "You will ride Buttons after your lesson," said Mr. Blake.

"After my lesson?" asked Mel.

"Yes," said Mr. Blake. "He needs the exercise, and you will be doing me a favor."

"He is such a nice man," said Mel later.

"But what about this?" Mother said to Mr. Blake.

"She is a special one," said Mr. Blake. "And it's true, that pony gets fat and devilish, and not many children can ride him. He does not really earn his keep."

So it was arranged. Mel would have her lesson, and then she was free, with Buttons, just the two of them.

"But it is not fair," Mother told Mr. Blake. "You still

have to feed him. If Mel rides him, why can't she work for his keep?"

"Perhaps she could," said Mr. Blake. There were saddles to soap and blankets to mend, and always there were stalls to clean and feed to measure and carry, and the stable yard to rake clean. "Two hours a day should pay his keep," said Mr. Blake.

So Mel was gone all day—from sunup until she came home at dinnertime, smelling of horse and happy.

The family would see her again at breakfast briefly, smelling of horses still, then off she would go with Jeff to fill water buckets; to carry pitchforks of hay and straw, clumsily yet; to measure oats and clean stalls. All the stable-boys helped her; all of them liked her, and Jeffy, too. He was accepted by the stable dogs, and could come and go as he pleased.

"You ride that black mare this morning," Mr. Blake would say; whichever horse did not suit the class, Mel got. And she got special attention. Sometimes she even helped the little ones.

But though the stableboys liked Mel, the little girls who came for lessons did not. "She's too smart," they would say. "She's snooty. She thinks she knows so much." They watched her ride away after class on Buttons, and it soon got around that she was teacher's pet.

"She needs a good lesson," said one of the older girls. "Who does she think she is, anyway?"

"What kind of a lesson?" said another, grinning.

"I don't know. Let's meet after class over there behind the trailers and decide."

There were five of them. Three older than Mel, two the same age, all jealous. "I think we should put a bucket of water over that horse's stall so it will fall on her," said one.

"It might just fall on the horse," said another.

"We could cut her girth almost in two," said a third. "I read a book once where . . ."

"That would be too dangerous," said the most sensible one. "We don't want to kill her." They all giggled.

"What is it they put under a saddle?" asked the smallest girl. "To make a horse buck?"

"A burr," said one. "I know where there is a burr bush. You must dry them to make them prickly."

And so it was arranged. Warm with anticipation, the little girls smiled and went to meet their mothers.

Chapter 7

When Mel began to be gone all day, Zee Zee found herself drawn to the attic. As she sat cross-legged among the boxes, trying little pieces of this and that together, dreaming in the warm shaft of sunlight, ideas began to take shape and people the attic with their beings. But still she could not decide what to make. "There is too much," said Zee Zee. "Too many lovely things. It is impossible to decide."

"Yes," said Mother, "I know."

But finally Zee Zee did decide, and this is how it happened.

In the park, besides the zoo, there were several museums. First, there was the Museum of Natural History, then the aquarium, and farther away, the art museums. In one of these, Zee Zee made her decision.

"There is a new exhibit of crafts, of furniture and tapestries and handmade rugs," said Mother. They did not go to the opening, for that was at night, with champagne. "And not for children," said Mother. "Also, too crowded to see." They went when there would be no crowd, early the next morning, Linda and Deb, Zee Zee and Mother. Mel was too busy; much too busy, as they were to find out later.

When Zee Zee walked into the gallery she was overwhelmed. Color and texture cascaded and shimmered from every side. The light from the glass ceiling made jewels of the colors; the textures of wool and wood, of yarn and clay and enameled metal had to be felt, even though Zee Zee knew she shouldn't. Leather lay softly on handmade rosewood furniture; tapestries hung, glowing, before her; handmade rugs had to have hands thrust deep into their thick, yarny surfaces. Zee Zee thought of her own colors and textures at home. I want to make all of these, she thought, all of them. Everything. She was dizzy with the thought, with the longing of it.

Linda and Deb and Mother were wandering over the gallery, each looking in her own way. Zee Zee needed to go and sit quietly by herself and think. Through a little door she glimpsed a white marble bench. Here she would sit alone for a little while.

As she entered the doorway a whole new beautiful sight confronted her. It was a small square room—but not a room. It was a garden in the center of the museum, surrounded by high walls. It was lighted with daylight from a glass ceiling. A fountain splashed into a marble pool. Potted trees and flowering bushes stood about in tubs. The water made patterns of light on the walls.

A garden inside of a house—why, one could have this right in the city. Snug between ugly buildings, you could have a garden house.

How dismal their old apartment had been, drab and closed and sunless. The best place of all had been the roof, where you could see the sky.

If one must live in the city, Zee Zee thought, this is the kind of house to have. The garden would be two stories high. Here, on this side, a kitchen would open into it. Next to that, a library with a fireplace. Above them would be a bedroom with a balcony looking down on the garden. On the other side, a bedroom below; another balconied one above.

The ceiling would be glass. There would be bright tapestries on the walls, real trees in mosaic pots, handmade quilts on the beds, carved doors for the library.

There would be hammocks in the garden. And wide smooth walks. From the bedrooms spiral stairways would lead to the roof, where there would be roof gardens.

It will be easy to make a model, Zee Zee thought. And there it was, the decision made. The house would contain all the rugs, the tapestries, the sculpture that she had thought of making. From the glass roof, a flight of carved birds would descend. The doors would be inlaid with colored woods and mosaic. Carved animals would decorate the balcony railings.

In the quiet attic the house would grow, a house within a house, the sun shining through the glass roof.

Zee Zee sat quite still, thinking of the house, her face warmed by the sun, her hands clasped tightly together.

This was the way Mother found her, sitting small and still by the fountain, lost in a world of her own. Mother went away without being seen.

Finally, Zee Zee had thought enough. The idea was set in her mind. There was no danger of forgetting it, of losing the dream. It was part of her. And she was terribly hungry —starving. Her stomach growled loudly.

The four of them ate double hamburgers covered with onions and thick tomatoes and mustard, and then they walked in the park among the rustle of summer leaves, dreamy and contented, their world a lovely place, all unaware that the world was a hateful place for Mel just then.

"We'll do it right before class," said the oldest of the five girls. "She always helps saddle the horses, as if we couldn't saddle our own."

"You do it, Clara, you're the tallest," said one. So Clara hung back, then, seeing which horse was left for Mel, walked quickly toward it.

Quickly it was done, with no one the wiser. The saddle was not heavy enough to push the burr into the horse's back until Mel's weight was on it. The horse was a big, rawboned pinto, ugly of disposition, not much liked. The little girls smiled and rode, single file, into the ring.

Mel had one foot in the stirrup, and her weight on it. Up went her leg, over the cantle—and the next thing she knew she was sitting flat on the ground, the big pinto snorting and bucking at the end of the reins.

Mr. Blake came running. He grabbed the pinto, jerked him once, and began to back him, running, slapping him across the chest with a rope halter. The pinto rolled his eyes and ran backward, more frightened of Mr. Blake than hurt by the burr.

Mel got up and stood bewildered, her face very red. Mr. Blake stopped finally, and the pinto stood trembling, eyes still rolling. Mr. Blake put his foot in the stirrup and was in the saddle before the horse could get the first buck out. It wasn't much of a buck—the pinto was too afraid of Mr. Blake—but he crouched and trembled in a most peculiar way.

Immediately Mr. Blake eased his weight off the saddle, leaning on one hand on the horse's withers. The pinto sighed in relief. Mr. Blake swung to the ground, and with one motion loosened the girth. He felt under the saddle. Then he looked hard at the stableboys, who had gathered to watch. They look chagrined and angry.

The little girls looked innocent. Now all in the ring, riding around and around, they looked very innocent indeed.

Mr. Blake removed the burr, rubbed the pinto's back tenderly, tightened the girth, and handed the reins to Mel. She got on.

Mr. Blake walked into the ring. He did not say a word. He beckoned to the first little girl coming around. Her face was pink. When she stopped beside him, he merely motioned. She dismounted. He pointed to the gate.

Soon Mr. Blake was holding twelve sets of reins. Twelve quiet horses stood around him. Twelve pink-faced little girls flocked together outside the ring, missing their lesson.

Mr. Blake got his own big Thoroughbred, Rambler, and off he and Mel went together down the trail, Jeff and two Dalmatians tagging along behind.

The next class, there were five apologies from the five guilty girls, who, unwillingly, perhaps untruthfully, but quite properly, told Mel how sorry they were. Mr. Blake listened while they did.

Chapter 8

Mother was starting illustrations for a new book. She had received the galleys, and she read aloud from them to the children each night.

They would gather around the fire after dinner, sprawled and clustered, mostly on the floor, Panda and Jeffy, too, and hear a chapter. Deb would lie curled on the couch, eyes closed, thinking what pictures she would make for it. Linda would lie by the fire, eyes closed, too, but wondering, wondering if she could write like that. "Read that part again," Linda would say, and Mother would go back, much to everyone's annoyance. Finally, Linda would take part of the galleys to bed, to read over and over again. "She makes it sound so lovely," she would say, "with so few words."

Mother, too, would take part of the galleys to bed.

Notebook and sketchbook and a green jar full of sharpened pencils stood on her night table. She would prop herself up in bed and read and reread and make notes and sketches, until the people in the story were alive and moving on the pages, the trees really growing, the animals with personalities of their own.

Mother's bed, like Mel's, was by her window. She, too, liked to look out at the night-park, at the trees wrapped in mist, at the silvered bridle trail on moonlit nights, at an occasional squirrel lurking in the path. On misty nights she could see strange shapes in the wisps of fog, strange new landscapes for her books.

One night the park was like a white desert, chilled under a frozen sky, only here and there a barren rock rising. The fog lay thick and deep, the low moon round and white as ice. When Mother looked again there was a silhouette against the moon. She caught her breath and stared. Was she having hallucinations?

The horse was very far away, but she could see him plainly. He stood for a long time, neck arched and mane blowing in the fog, looking over the misty expanse much as she was doing.

The fog began to rise and swirl in gusts. Soon most of the hill was exposed. The stallion stood very still. As the moon rose he turned slowly from silhouette to a pale, misty gray. Then something dark stirred below him on the hill, and he was gone.

Mother wiped her eyes, wondering if she had been asleep.

"Does Mr. Blake keep some of his horses in the pasture?" Mother asked Mel the next morning.

"He doesn't have any pasture," said Mel.

"Not even in the park?" asked Mother. "Can't he even pasture some in the park?"

"No," said Mel. "The zoo has some places for antelope, and a few deer and sheep, I think. But no horses. There are no horses in the park." Mel was quiet a minute. "Did you see a horse?" she asked.

"Well," said Mother, "I think I did. But it was dark, and foggy, and . . ."

"What color?" asked Mel, excited.

"Gray, I think," said Mother.

"Tell me," Mel said, squirming, "when did you see it?"

Mel and Zee Zee were curled up on Mother's bed, barefoot and in pajamas. Mother began to tell them what she had seen.

Now three of them—if you counted Jeffy—had seen the ghost. "I'm sure he saw something," said Mel.

"Do you think it was a ghost?" whispered Zee Zee.

"It was something." Mother was whispering too. "Ghost or real, it was something."

"Let's go look," Mel said eagerly.

"It's too sunny," Zee Zee reminded her. "We won't see it now."

"We might see hoofprints," said Mel.

"But how could you tell?" asked Mother. "With all the horses that go about in the park?"

"Yes," said Mel, "that's true. But if it's a wild horse," she continued, "it won't have shoes."

"Can you tell by the prints?" asked Zee Zee.

"I think so," said Mel.

"If it's a ghost," said Zee Zee, "it won't have prints at all."

"Well, let's get dressed and go," said Mother, getting out of bed.

"I'll bring something to eat," whispered Mel as she tumbled out the door.

"Be careful what it is," said Mother. "I don't want pickles for breakfast. And put the kettle on."

While Zee Zee dressed she looked in at the bare table, standing alone in the big attic. I will start today, she thought. Then the ghost pulled her away, and down the ladder she pelted to find hoofprints or to find none where some should be.

The fog had gone, and the morning park was crisp, with sharp shadows.

"It was just here," said Mother, pointing to a little hill. "I'm sure it was."

They searched the hill inch by inch, but it was very grassy. They found nothing except one small mark in a patch of mud. "It could be," said Mel, "but I can't tell for sure."

"Well, then," said Mother as they sat eating jellied rolls, "perhaps we have seen a ghost after all."

"I wish I had seen it," said Zee Zee.

"But people don't believe in ghosts," said Mel.

"I guess not," said Mother, "but what is one to do?"

Chapter 9

Mel's leg was bruised from her fall. Though she didn't bother much about it, it looked horrid. It had turned quite purple in four big splotches below the knee and had ugly red scrape marks as well, so that in a dress she was an interesting sight. When Aunt Vivian saw it there was no stopping her questions until she found out what had happened. The minute Mother said "Horse," Aunt Vivian leaned over and took a great whiff of Mel and swore that she smelled monstrous (perhaps her sweater did smell a bit horsy).

When Aunt Vivian found out Mel was riding every day, and cleaning stalls, too—"You didn't *have* to tell her that," said Mel later—she was livid.

Zee Zee and Linda held each other and giggled behind the kitchen door, but Mel stood beside Mother, still as a mouse. Spencer came in in the middle of the harangue, and even he was quiet. Mother's eyes got darker and darker, but she said nothing. Mel held her breath and glared.

Afterward there was really nothing to say. Linda made cocoa, and they all sat around the kitchen table. Mel was ready to cry, she was so angry, but Mother only smiled. "She's just unhappy herself," said Mother. "Don't let her spoil things for you. I think you smell rather nice."

"Not as nice as snakes," said Spence.

"Ugh," said Zee Zee.

"I wish Aunt Kelly were here," said Mother.

"What would she have done?" asked Linda.

"I don't really know," said Mother, "but you can bet it would have been worth seeing."

It was then that the banging on the door silenced them all. Could it be Aunt Vivian, come back?

"That was a man's knock," said Spence.

Jeff barked wildly until he was close to the door and could sniff under it. Then he wagged his tail.

At first Mel saw only a pair of wrinkled boots. Then she recognized the familiar Levi's above them and the plain shirt, and saw a quiet worried face. How strange to see Mr. Blake in their own kitchen; the place did not seem to fit him as the stable did. Something was wrong. And his expression was wrong. He looked angry—worried.

"It's Buttons," cried Mel. "Oh, what has happened? Please, Mr. Blake, what has happened?"

"He's out," said Mr. Blake simply, still standing in the doorway. "The little devil has gotten out." He was to use worse language before the night was over, some of which the children would cherish guiltily and use in secret sometimes.

"Those girls didn't do it! Oh, they couldn't!" cried Mel.

"No," said Mr. Blake, "I don't think so. He's been chewing his door bolt; there are teeth marks on it."

Mel grabbed her sweater and nearly knocked Mr. Blake down trying to get through the door.

"Wait, now," said Mr. Blake, holding her back. "I have two horses saddled outside, and the boys are already looking. Can anyone else ride?"

No one spoke. "Then," said Mr. Blake, "would you walk down the highway, and try to keep him from getting onto it?" They all nodded.

"Stay between the street and the pony," said Mr. Blake. "Spread out, and if you see him, don't let him get beyond you. Wave and shout if you're sure you can drive him back into the park. If he gets by you, don't chase him, just be still, don't drive him further into the city."

Into the city! Mel heard it with a chill: the cars, the slippery concrete, the traffic; the trucks and freeways, the terrible hard pavement where a little horse could slip and fall, could break his leg, could be caught in bright headlights and panicked, could be hit and crippled by a screeching truck. She was in a frenzy to get out and look for him.

Mr. Blake had brought the big Thoroughbred mare. For a moment Mel wished it were Patsy, a friend, at such a time. But the big mare was faster, and handy.

"The boys are at the back side of the park," said Mr. Blake. "We'll work into the valley first."

Mel and Mr. Blake crossed the street close together, the

horses snorting and fussing as the dusk and fog settled around them. By the time they were on the park trail it was almost completely dark. Mel could see very little.

"There will be a moon soon," said Mr. Blake. "Where would he go, Mel? Does he have a favorite spot, somewhere he wants to roll or graze?"

Mel thought about it. Yes, there was a favorite spot. The park was so strange at night that she felt quite turned around for a minute, but then she headed toward the big old willow tree at the far end of the valley. Whispering and trying to hold the spooky mare steady in the dark, Mel told Mr. Blake how Buttons always wanted to graze just beside the tree. Many times she had taken a halter with her so that he could crop the soft grass while she lay beside him and watched the clouds drift by.

The moon was beginning to rise, and the pale fog was lifting, so that now they could see each other. It seemed strange to see a Western saddle on Mr. Blake's big bay Thoroughbred. A lariat lay loosely in Mr. Blake's hand. Rambler was watching the willow tree—or something by it—with ears pricked forward. So was Lucy, snorting softly. Mr. Blake pulled Rambler to a slower walk and looked hard at the ground beneath the tree. "Let's stay here a minute, until the moon is brighter." He settled Rambler down and leaned forward, peering intently into the dark.

Soon the valley was palely lighted, the meadow gleaming white and ghostly, the willow limbs shining silver like the locks of a giant.

"Now, Mel," said Mr. Blake, "ride in there and see if you can rustle anything out."

The mare side-stepped and snorted at the dark place under the tree, but Mel edged her closer, staring hard into the shadows.

Suddenly, right at the edge of the shadow, the mare stopped, planted her feet, and snorted loudly. She backed a few steps and tried to whirl away. Mel held her steady.

"Go on in," Mr. Blake directed.

She kicked the mare forward, still snorting and trying to lunge. As they drew into the shadow the mare seemed to be eyeing something. Mel gave her a good slap with the reins, and in they went. There was a faint noise to one side, then silence.

The mare seemed steadier now. Mel made her move through the dark and into the thicket beyond. All through the thicket they went, shadows playing tricks. Several times she saw dark horse shapes, only to find they were bushes.

When they returned to Mr. Blake, his rope still held ready, he had seen nothing. He looked puzzled and annoyed. "There was something in there all right. He's slipped around us, the little beggar."

Mel was close to tears. She was frightened for the little horse, and she was angry, too. It was dark and cold and hard to see. What a devil that pony was, what an uncaring little devil; he didn't mind at all that she was worried sick about him, afraid he might be hurt.

No, Buttons didn't care. Not one bit. He only switched his tail and tossed his head and watched Mel ride about in the thicket, finding nothing.

He had heard the horses coming from a long way off. Standing quietly under the tree, he had waited until they got quite close. When Mel rode into the shadow he watched her, a devilish gleam in his eye. When she had got

close enough, he moved off slowly into the thicket, then skirted the valley, a shadow moving in shadows, and climbed the little hill.

Now he was standing in another thicket, watching the valley below. The moonlight picked out the two riders on the silvered meadow, but Buttons, in the inky thicket, was just another shadow.

It was a fine night. Buttons had already grazed his fill of the good green grass, topping off a meal of oats and hay. He had not got out of his stall until after feeding time had come and gone, and the stables were deserted and still.

A very fine night. The moon beamed down on the riders below, and once in a while a word or two of their conversation drifted up to him. Mr. Blake sounded very cross.

A drink would taste nice after the grass. Buttons decided he would meander over the hill to the little stream on the other side.

Quietly, softly, he backed out of the thicket. Gently, slowly, he skirted the hill above Mel and Mr. Blake. When he got over the rise of the hill, where he could not be seen, he put his ears back, switched his tail, and ran, half bucking, kicking his heels in pure devilment, down the other side.

Chapter 10

The pool and the little stream which fed it were silver in the moonlight. Where some broombushes grew close to the pool's edge Buttons slid quietly in, so that from above he was only another bush.

The water was cold and tasted of green things. It had flavors the stable water never had. He drank for a long time; then he playfully sloshed and pawed in the water. If it had not been so cold he would have rolled in it.

Suddenly he stopped still. From the opposite side of the park other horses were coming. He could hear them faintly far along the trail. Then one whinnied. There was another whinny, then a short human comment.

Buttons stood very still and listened. Behind him there was sudden galloping as Mr. Blake and Mel ascended the hill.

Buttons stayed where he was, ears twitching this way and that as the noises came from one side, then the other. When they got close enough he would slip away. But not yet. It was deliciously exciting to stand like a shadow and hear everyone thrashing about and making a great stir. He took another drink.

Then, right beside him, there was a rustling in the bushes. He whirled, ready to run. A gray, shaggy face looked out at him from beside the broombush. It was Jeffy.

Forgotten by everyone in the excitement, Jeffy had joined the chase in his own way. At first, staying close behind Zee Zee, he had gone down the street with the rest. But he could hear the horses and Mel's voice going toward the valley, and soon he began to follow them. Then a rabbit distracted him, and off he went on his own adventure. The rabbit—never really frightened—led him a merry chase, and Jeff, panting and cheated, finally lost him.

Disappointed, Jeff had started back toward Mel and Mr. Blake. But he was thirsty. First he would get a drink. When he neared the silver pool he smelled a friend there. How nice to find a companion having a quiet drink beside him.

They smelled noses and Buttons snorted gently. Jeff wagged his tail happily and Buttons switched his and shook his head. Prancing slightly, Buttons started off along the stream, clinging to the shadows, Jeff behind him. They could hear the riders plainly, moving to the spot where they had been. Jeff snuffled a little.

The riders were following close behind; a logical place to go, to the stream and down it. The horses were beginning to separate and spread out, to hem them in.

Quickly backtracking, Buttons slipped into a denser thicket, ducked low under some cypress trees, and with Jeff close on his heels, skirted a small lily pond. The ducks watched sleepily, but did not quack. They were used to horses, and best be silent with a dog nearby.

Around the pond and up another hill, gorse-covered. Now the sounds had died behind them, the others had lost them. How dull. Buttons turned and surveyed the scene below. The moon was now so bright that every detail was magnified. There they were, silly people, fanning out in a business-like manner around the spot he and Jeff had left. Buttons shook out his mane, stamped his feet, snorted at Jeff in a wild manner, and took off, running at dead speed up the hill in plain sight of them all—Jeffy close at his side—ears down in the wind and tail streaming.

By the time the others reached the top of the hill, riding hard with lariats held ready, Buttons had disappeared again. Some choice words exploded among the crew and they spread out once more.

Buttons and Jeffy went down another valley and, with burrs clinging to them, through another thicket. Then they stood still in the shadows, Jeffy panting, and stared out upon a garden of flowers.

Prize park flowers, all in neat beds, bloomed in great clumps before them. Nile lilies raised their round heads, fuchsia and honeysuckle waved gently, and dwarf trees posed like fairies in the moonlight.

Behind them they could hear the horses. Out into the garden they dashed, through the lilies and azaleas and the splendid camellia bushes, dodging and turning this way and

that, and into a clump of eucalyptus trees on the other side. But now the others were gaining; across the flower garden they came.

Buttons slipped through the trees that skirted the garden, back the way he had come, leaving the blowing horses behind him. Back up the hill he went, Jeffy close beside him. The fog was beginning to roll in on brisk breezes. Soon they would be hidden. As the fog swept around them they watched the riders below grow misty.

Suddenly, off to the right, farther up the hill, Buttons saw a movement. He whirled. There above them stood another horse. There was no rider on him. Buttons caught his scent and that made him cautious; it was a stallion. Head high, ready to run, the white stallion pawed once, snorted, then disappeared as mists covered him.

Curious and forgetting caution, Buttons advanced. Then suddenly there was a whirring by his ear, and a rope lay around Buttons's neck. He whirled to run, but he was not fast enough. He was snubbed up short to a tree, and a figure was walking toward him.

Zee Zee had grown tired of standing waiting in the street as she was told. When the chase came near to where she was and passed her, she crept closer to the park and finally entered it. As she topped a little hill she saw the riders come galloping, enter the flower garden, and return through it. What a mess, Zee Zee thought. Someone in the park will be angry.

Then a flash of movement caught her eye.

She looked across the valley to the hill opposite, where

fog was blowing. There, wrapped in mist, stood the ghost horse, pale as the mist itself. He made no sound. He tossed his head and pawed at the fog. The mists thickened, and he disappeared. Then they passed, and the bare hill stood empty.

But wait! Next to the trees farther down the hill, standing dark and real and tethered to a tree—pulling back, ears flat, fighting the rope—was Buttons.

The riders saw him, too. They came up around him on three sides. Mr. Blake untied him and rubbed his neck and talked to him until he was calm. Jeffy sat near him, tongue lolling, and beside him a sniffling Mel was dismounting. She hugged Buttons and scolded him. Buttons turned his head away, ears back, angry at being caught.

Someone else had been in the park! No one had seen him. No one but Buttons. Even if he could have told, he was shut in his stall in disgrace, both doors closed. "No hay, no grain, no water," Mr. Blake told the boys, "until I say so." A tear ran down Mel's cheek, but she needn't have bothered. Buttons didn't care. He had had a fine evening.

"It's made of horsehair," said Mr. Blake as Mel fingered the rope they had taken from Buttons's neck. It was braided into a pattern of white and gray, a round, firm rope, scratchy, but very strong.

"Horsehair?" asked Zee Zee.

"Yes," said Mr. Blake, and showed them how it was made. "It's a very fine one, too."

Chapter 11

Zee Zee could have told Mr. Blake about the ghost horse, but she did not. It was still a secret. She told Mother and Mel late that night. Snug on Mother's bed, warm inside with cocoa and wrapped in a quilt, she told them.

"But you didn't see a person?" asked Mel.

"No," said Zee Zee. "Could a ghost horse tie him up like that?"

"I think we have more than a ghost," said Mother, wiggling her toes farther under the quilt.

"Could it have been a real person, and a ghost horse?" Zee Zee really wanted it to be a ghost. "No horse could be so beautiful," she added.

Mel frowned.

"Are you sure there's no horse like that at the stables?" asked Mother.

"Yes," said Mel, "I'm sure. There's no white horse at all, except Patsy, and that wasn't Patsy, I know that much."

"Do you think we could find footprints in the morning?" asked Zee Zee.

"Probably plenty of them," Mother said, laughing. "Horse and man, too, right where the ghost was."

"Yes," the girls agreed. How could one ever tell which was which?

"There's no other stable near?" asked Mother.

"Oh, no," said Mel. "None at all. Anywhere."

"Hmmmm," said Mother. "May I tell Aunt Kelly about the ghost?"

"When is she coming?" both girls cried together.

"Morning after tomorrow," said Mother. "The telegram came this evening, but between Aunt Vivian and Buttons, I had no time to tell." She wriggled farther down under the covers. "Maybe Aunt Kelly could help solve the mystery."

"Or maybe she would put it in a book," said Mel.

"She might," said Mother.

"Tell her," agreed Zee Zee.

"Yes," said Mel, "if she's not like Aunt Vivian."

"But then we should tell Deb and Linda too," said Zee Zee. "And Spencer."

"He would only make fun," said Mel.

"It's not fair to make him the only one left out," said Mother.

"Then don't let's tell anyone yet," said Mel. It was her secret first, so they agreed.

"Poor Spence," said Mother.

"He has his snakes," said Zee Zee.

"Whoever wants to go meet Aunt Kelly," said Mother, "can have breakfast at the airport." So there was no one left at home but Panda and Jeffy, sitting side by side in the kitchen watching them go down the back steps to the garage.

"There will hardly be room for luggage," said Deb.

"She won't have much," said Mother. "Her boxes are being shipped."

"Shouldn't I stay and dust?" asked Linda.

"You wouldn't want to miss breakfast?" Mother asked. "You dusted yesterday."

"All right," said Linda, beaming.

Aunt Kelly had short red hair mottled with streaks of white. Piebald, thought Mel, not unkindly. She had freckles across her nose, like Mel, and her eyes were very blue.

"Blue eyes," said Zee Zee. "No one in our family has blue eyes." All were brown.

"Except Panda," said Mel.

"Yes," said Zee Zee.

"Who is Panda?" asked Aunt Kelly.

"Our cat," said Spence.

"Well, if he and I have matching eyes, perhaps we will be friends," said Aunt Kelly.

"Yes," said Zee Zee. She thought they would.

Breakfast was very fine, with sausage and eggs for Mel

and Deb and Linda, pancakes for Zee Zee, a hamburger for Spence, and French toast and honey for Mother. Aunt Kelly had pancakes and sausages and eggs.

"More coffee?" asked Mother.

"Oh, yes," said Aunt Kelly.

"Here is the park; it's just as your letter described," Aunt Kelly said, leaning from the car window. "Look at the azaleas. And there is a squirrel."

"Where, where?" whispered Mel, outdone.

"There," said Aunt Kelly, pointing. There was.

When they arrived home the dog and cat, shut in, were waiting with hurt looks, but cozy, Zee Zee noticed. "I am sorry," Aunt Kelly said to them formally. "It was entirely my fault. Will you forgive me?"

They did, wagging and purring respectively.

"It is lovely," said Aunt Kelly of the old house. "It is a fine house for a family."

"Come and see your apartment," Mel said proudly. "We painted it all, and it has new . . ."

"Let her see for herself," said Deb. "You'll spoil it, Mel."

"All right," said Mel, but it was hard to do.

From her living-room window Aunt Kelly, too, could see the park. "I can lie here eating bonbons, and watch Mel ride down the trail," she said, curling up on the blue couch. There were books on the shelves; each child had chosen a few.

Facing the couch were two high-backed red chairs. Beside the fireplace was a basket of wood. "I can see the fire from my bed," said Aunt Kelly, delighted. Mother had placed the bed so.

There was a red lacquered table in the kitchen, again looking on the park, and a large white-enameled pot for coffee.

Beside the couch there was an ample desk, and in the center of this a typewriter and a great stack of white paper, unused and gleaming. Aunt Kelly hugged Mother. "It was Linda's idea," said Mother. Aunt Kelly hugged Linda, harder.

"It's what I'd want," said Linda.

"Yes," said Aunt Kelly, "it's what I *do* want. Just."

Dinner was more talk than food, and there was plenty of that, certainly. Linda had stuffed cabbage leaves with meat and onions; Deb had cooked rice with mushrooms and little peppers; Mother had tossed a salad, green and light; Zee Zee had made ginger cookies; and Mel had gathered water cress, illegally, in the park, having great trouble keeping Buttons out of it while she picked.

After dinner Spence showed his snakes to Aunt Kelly.

"How often do they eat?" asked Aunt Kelly.

"Oh, every two weeks or so," said Spence offhandedly, shrugging. "Whenever I can get mice for them."

"Why don't you raise mice?" asked Aunt Kelly practically.

"I did," said Spence, looking guiltily at Mother, "but they got away when we moved. Now I have to buy them. The girls don't like it."

That was true, they didn't.

"He can't have the mice in my attic," said Zee Zee.

They showed Aunt Kelly the house, each room straightened and scrubbed for the occasion. Linda's room, white and cool and plain, looked out through a sparkling window to a maple tree close enough to touch. Beneath the window stood a desk, huge and painted blue. On this desk, too, there was a typewriter and a stack of plain white paper. There was a bed also, of course, and a small chest of drawers and a cushioned chair, but mostly there was desk. And books. Rows and rows of white bookshelves over the bed and dresser, between the door and closet, filled to overflowing with books and books and more books.

"Ah," said Aunt Kelly, and smiled.

The attic was last. Aunt Kelly climbed the ladder. She gazed at the lovely rafters; she looked out at the moon and the sea. She opened the window. She breathed the salt air. She sighed. She listened to the night noises. This time she said, "Mmmm."

She climbed the little steps to the big attic behind Zee Zee and stood quite still while Zee Zee pulled the cord for the light.

Zee Zee had put the old table in the center of the room and placed a small chair before it. There was a big piece of plywood on the table for the floor of the house, and next to this were laid out, in neat rows, pencils, ruler, triangle and square, cutting knives, scissors, glue and sandpaper, paint brushes, empty jars, everything. Behind the chair, and beside it, clustered the boxes and trunks, the wood, the plastic, the cloth, glass mosaics, yarn, and small, flat stones for the fireplace.

The plan had been drawn, first on paper, then on plywood.

"Will it be to scale?" practical Deb had asked.

"Yes," Zee Zee had said, "an inch to the foot."

She would build the walls of balsa, studs in the center and balsa sheeting on both sides, she explained to Aunt Kelly. Heavy balsa beams lay ready, with plastic sheeting for the windows.

"I will hinge the end walls," said Zee Zee, "and part of this side wall, so I can see inside." She told Aunt Kelly how it would be, about the garden, about making a garden house in the city.

"I would like that," said Aunt Kelly. "I would like that very much." She half-closed her eyes, seeing the garden house as it would be.

"Would you really?" asked Zee Zee.

"Yes, I would," said Aunt Kelly. She was sitting on an upturned box, imagining the little house sitting on the table, and making herself small enough to go inside.

How different she is from Aunt Vivian, thought Zee Zee. Aunt Kelly's hair was mussed, her eyes bright, and her fingernails clean and plain. Aunt Vivian's nails were always painted, her wrinkles too powdered, and her hair too proper and stiff. Aunt Vivian's hair had a decided blue cast to it.

"Dye," said Spencer.

"No, only rinse," said Mother.

Zee Zee wanted very badly to tell Aunt Kelly about the

ghost. She wished they had not agreed to keep the secret quite so secret. What harm would it do? But she had promised.

Only she did wish that she could.

Chapter 12

Zee Zee need not have bothered wishing. She might have guessed that Aunt Kelly would find out soon enough for herself.

Aunt Kelly was a walk-in-the-woods person, a wander-in-the-fog person, and an even earlier riser than Mel was. One might know she would see the ghost. But it was not in the park that she saw it.

Aunt Kelly favored the beach for early-morning walks. She liked to hear the seals bark on the seal rock, early, when the sounds carried well. She liked to search the sand for shells, and see silver fish jump in the waves. She liked the early-morning colors on the water, and she liked the beach lonely and quiet, with only birds to share it.

Aunt Kelly stood alone at the edge of the sand, watching sandpipers dance along the foam. The ocean was still black

and wild. There was a ragged clump of rocks near the water, shoulder-high and hardly distinguishable from the dark sky. Aunt Kelly sat on them near where a wave was breaking and breathed the salty smell deeply. She could not be seen. It was so dark she looked like another lump on the rocks.

The air was very still. A curlew cried. A gull answered. But the ocean was the only real sound. Then something else was pounding like the ocean. Hoofs were beating down the sand behind her.

Down the horse came, near to the water, swerving around the rock, mane flying, silver tail flowing, pale and ghostly in the darkness. A pale figure clung low on his back. Quickly the hoofbeats were muffled in the dark and the figures disappeared. The surf lapped over the hoofprints, destroying them. The beach was quiet.

Whatever had been there was gone.

"A ghost horse. A ghostly white horse," whispered Aunt Kelly. She sat staring into the dark, but he did not come back.

Soon a great wave broke and made the rock she was sitting on an island, the water receding with a sucking noise. The tide is coming in, thought Aunt Kelly. I had better get off of here before I'm stranded. And she thought how funny it would be, when the sun rose and people started coming to the beach, to see an old, streaked-haired lady sitting on a rock in the middle of the ocean.

Perhaps there was something about the white ghost that made people want to keep him secret; or perhaps it was only the people themselves.

Aunt Kelly loved a secret thing, to share only with herself. Of course she loved her nieces too, and her nephew and her sister, and loved to share with them, but it was such a lovely thing to have a secret to share only with herself. For a little while she would keep it for her own. Perhaps she felt this way because she was a writer. It's hard to say. But she liked to hold a secret thing up and look at it, weave a story around it, imagine things about it, and it all seemed to spill away if she told it too soon.

Chapter 13

The old house's summer sounds, its faint groanings and
shiftings, blended with and became part of the family
noises as everyone settled in and the balmy days passed.
On a hot, quiet summer afternoon, sun drenching its roof,
the steady woodpecker-sound of Aunt Kelly's typewriter
droned with the house noises through the long afternoon.
On the next floor, along with the dull humming of the
refrigerator and the whisper of the water heater, another
typewriter muttered; this one more erratic, slower, hesi-
tating, then rushing ahead madly. Often, attracted by the
noise, Panda would come to sit on Linda's bed.

In the hall the clock ticked steadily, and upstairs in the
studio the swish of the mat knife cutting board and the
chink of the paper-cutter broke the stillness; the swoosh
of the charcoal fixative with which Mother sprayed her

drawings made a little exclamation. All these sounds became part of the old house just as the family had.

In the attic the little garden house was growing. Slice of a little knife cutting wood, shoosh of sandpaper, snip of scissors. Sun streamed warmly down, dust spattered, from the window, through the roof of the little house. A little house within a house, thought Zee Zee.

Mother had helped her with the framing. This was the hardest part. "If your angles aren't exact," said Mother, "and it's not quite square, things will never go right." Together they had got the main studs set, checking with square and level, and now the house stood, framed and strong, waiting for its walls to be sided. It looks, Zee Zee thought, like a real house being built.

Frosted plastic made the end walls. "For light," said Zee Zee, "but not for view." These walls looked to the street and the alley. "Or where street and alley would be," Zee Zee explained.

The roof was beamed and crossbeamed into little squares, and waited for its glass. This afternoon Zee Zee was covering the side walls with sheets of balsa, pinning them in place while the glue dried. The inside would be sanded smooth and painted white, like the garden room in the museum. She already knew how the tapestries would look, and the little trees.

She had sorted the small mosaic tiles and set aside enough for the patio floor. She had two sets, one rust-colored clay, the other deep-blue glass. She couldn't decide which she liked best. "I think the clay," said Zee Zee,

sticking pins. Her fingers were getting sore from the pins, but she would not use a thimble.

The only noises which stood out distinctly, not humming along with the rest, were Spencer's.

This afternoon the stair and hall had shook with shouting and running, and now Spencer's room seethed with small boys, all noisy and wiggly—only five, really, but seeming like a hundred. Two had snakes, one a large lizard.

"If we had a .22 we could shoot chipmunks in the park to feed them," one boy was saying.

"They wouldn't eat them dead," scoffed another.

"We could just stun them," said Spencer.

They all agreed it was a good idea, but did anyone have a .22? They had to admit, ashamed, that no one did. Misunderstood, not trusted by their parents, they were not allowed to have guns. Their determination in the face of hardship was touching, and vociferous.

Mel was learning to jump. Every afternoon she had a lesson on Rambler. "Buttons is too contrary to teach you properly," said Mr. Blake. And he was right, as usual. Buttons didn't care a fig if Mel learned anything; all he cared about was devilment and nonsense. Besides, after Mel and he had spent the morning in the park, he was ready for a nap, and stood drowsing in his stall, sleepily switching flies, while Mel had her lesson.

Sometimes there were little girls watching. Mel wished they would go away. They were not rude to her; they had learned they had better not be. But they were not friendly either, and Mel did not like them watching. She liked her lessons in peace, and the girls distracted her. "Stop thinking about them and pay attention," Mr. Blake said. And so she did.

"Poof on them," said Mel to herself, and went on about her business. Mr. Blake raised the bar a little.

Chapter 14

So the summer progressed, each one doing what she or he liked best. "We must have Aunt Vivian to dinner to meet Aunt Kelly," said Mother, breaking the peace and perfection of the days.

"Must we?" said Zee Zee and Mel together. "Must we?"

"Yes," said Mother, "it would be rude not to."

"I don't care," said Mel.

"It should be very interesting," said Mother.

Yes, it should be that all right.

"And it's only for dinner," said Mother.

The table was laid in the dining room with a cloth as blue as the bachelor buttons arranged in the center. Pale-green candles stood in tall brass holders, and the plates were bordered in green. The napkins were pale green, too.

Linda had done the table. She hoped Aunt Kelly would like it—she had done it for her.

There was a fire blazing merrily. "A fire in the middle of summer?" Aunt Vivian said, shocked. Aunt Vivian had worn her fur coat, though. She laid it over a chair until after Aunt Kelly had been introduced. Then she asked Linda to hang it up.

"I understand you write books," said Aunt Vivian bluntly when they were seated by the fire.

"Yes, I do," said Aunt Kelly, petting Jeffy.

"Then you were in Germany doing research, I presume," continued Aunt Vivian, frowning at Jeff.

"A writer does research wherever she goes," said Aunt Kelly, smiling directly at Aunt Vivian.

Aunt Vivian paused for a minute, dusting lint from her skirt. "What sort of books do you write?" she asked. "Perhaps I may have read some of them."

"I write books about people," said Aunt Kelly. "And books about animals, too," she continued, smiling at Jeffy. "I write books for children. I doubt you have read them."

"And you are published, I suppose?"

"Well, no," said Aunt Kelly, smiling. "But my books are." There was a little silence. "Would you like a little sherry before dinner?" asked Aunt Kelly, taking the tray from Linda as she entered.

"Why, yes," said Aunt Vivian, "I believe I would. Thank you."

"I think," said Linda in the kitchen, "that Aunt Vivian likes Aunt Kelly!" Mother raised an eyebrow. She was dressing the salad. "I think Aunt Kelly outmatches her," said Linda, delighted. Mother smiled. "I think," said Linda, "that Aunt Vivian is impressed."

"Come on," said Mother, taking a tray, "let's not miss the fun."

At dinner Aunt Vivian found her manners long enough to praise the chicken and even admire the table, though offhandedly.

"It's lovely," said Aunt Kelly, smiling at Linda. "And the chicken is delicious." She smiled over Linda's shoulder at Jeffy and Panda, who had been banned from the dining room and who sat shoulder to shoulder on the threshold of the kitchen, yearning. Aunt Vivian could not see them.

"And what have you done with your summer?" Aunt Vivian was asking Zee Zee. "Playing in the park, I suppose?"

"Well, yes," said Zee Zee, not wanting to share her summer with Aunt Vivian.

"And Melani," continued Aunt Vivian, "have you been playing in the park, too?" She knew perfectly well what Mel had been doing.

"I think," said Aunt Kelly, "that the girls are a little too old to be playing."

Before Aunt Vivian could say, "But what else could children of that age do but play?"—which was exactly what she was going to say—Aunt Kelly continued. "Certainly, if I were spending my summer as they are, I would not call it play."

Aunt Vivian, looking blank, finally got the idea. "I hardly know what you mean," she said, knowing perfectly well. "Surely you are not implying that Melani is still allowed to go about at that stable, with those rough men and unwholesome language." Mel giggled, then looked stricken.

Aunt Vivian didn't seem to notice. She went right on, well in her stride: "And certainly you must have a great deal of time for play, being a writer. What do you do to keep yourself busy?"

Aunt Kelly only laughed, giving Aunt Vivian a charming smile.

Why, thought Zee Zee quite suddenly and unexpectedly, Aunt Vivian is jealous. She's jealous of all of us. And Zee Zee began to look at Aunt Vivian in a new way, and to wonder how Aunt Vivian spent her days.

"Perhaps," said Mel later, "she doesn't like her own company."

"How too bad, if that is true," said Linda.

"What does Aunt Vivian do?" asked Zee Zee.

"She works, you know," said Mother, "in a very nice shop. But her evenings are lonely, I'm sure."

"But what else does she do?" pursued Zee Zee.

"You mean," said Mother, "what does she really enjoy?"

"I guess I do," said Zee Zee.

"I don't know," said Mother. "I don't believe I ever heard her say she enjoyed anything."

Deb and Linda were taking up the plates. Spencer is certainly squirming, thought Zee Zee. Mother was putting on the dessert. "This is Vivian's recipe," she was saying to Aunt Kelly as she set a shimmering chocolate mousse in front of Aunt Vivian for her to serve. "Of course, I

don't make it as well as Vivian"—Mother smiled at Aunt
Kelly—"but it is such an excellent recipe, I wanted you
to taste it."

Spencer squirmed again. Zee Zee frowned at him. "Why,
but publishing a book is mostly luck," Aunt Vivian was
saying as they took their coffee in by the fire. Deb and
Linda were clearing the table.

"There's luck in everything," said Aunt Kelly smoothly.
"Meeting an old friend unexpectedly on the street, having
it not rain when you plan a picnic, seeing a ghost—what's
that but luck, tell me?"

The girls were silent, staring.

"But surely you don't believe in ghosts!" Aunt Vivian said.

Spencer, on the couch, squirmed again, and wiggled. Mother glared at him. "But of course," said Aunt Kelly. "I enjoy the thought. And who's to say? Perhaps one day I shall meet one." She sipped her coffee, watching Spencer over her cup, and glancing at Mother.

Mother looked curiously at Aunt Kelly, frowned again at Spencer, and motioned all three children to get started on the dishes. Spencer should have been eager to go, but somehow he was not. "Perhaps he's growing fond of Aunt Vivian," whispered Mel as she and Zee Zee went ahead. Zee Zee looked over her shoulder to see Spencer squirming again, furtively, and looking more uncomfortable.

"I believe he has a snake with him," gasped Zee Zee. "Oh, my, what if Aunt Vivian sees it?" This sent them into fits of muffled giggling behind the closed kitchen door.

Finally, after a sharp word from Mother, Spencer joined them. Both girls fixed him with a cold stare. "Do you have a snake down here?" Zee Zee asked.

Spencer looked sullen. "I did have," he said finally.

They waited—two accusing sisters, staring.

"It got out of my pocket," said Spence.

"Where?" said Zee Zee, grabbing his arm with a soapy hand. "My gosh, Spencer, where is it?"

Spencer, shaking his arm loose, only growled. Girls always got so excited.

"Where is it?" repeated Zee Zee.

"It won't come out while so many people are there," said Spence.

"But where?" asked Zee Zee and Mel together.

Spencer only looked more sullen, and picked up a pan to dry.

"It's in the couch, isn't it?" whispered Mel.

Spencer looked at his shoes.

"Well, is it?" insisted Zee Zee.

"Yes," said Spence miserably.

Mel's eyes got very big. "Then Aunt Vivian is sitting on it." She dissolved into fits of laughter, clinging to Zee Zee.

"My gosh," said Spencer. One minute they were mad, the next minute having laughing fits. "My gosh, what if she hurts it?" he said indignantly.

"Hadn't we better tell Mother?" Zee Zee said, trying to be serious.

"You would!" said Spence. "Girls!"

"But Spencer, what if it comes out?" asked Mel. This started them laughing again, clinging helplessly to each other.

Finally Spencer agreed.

The only way Mother could think of to get Aunt Vivian out of the room was to show her the new book illustrations. "Why, yes," said Aunt Vivian unexpectedly, "I should like to see them."

I do believe she is lonely, thought Zee Zee again. She only wants to share. Zee Zee felt ashamed.

Chapter 15

As soon as the grownups were out of the room, the children pulled the cushions off the couch. Spencer felt into the cracks as far as he could. The girls would not. "Won't he bite?" asked Mel.

"How else am I to get him out?" said Spence with a growl. He could feel nothing. "We'll have to turn the couch over," he decided, "and get in at the back."

It was heavy, but with Linda and Deb they managed. The back was upholstered, too. "Get a screwdriver," said Linda, "and pliers." There were footsteps in the hall above.

"They're coming back," gasped Mel.

"Not so soon," whispered Zee Zee. There was nothing to do except go on. But it was only Aunt Kelly.

"She's getting restless," said Aunt Kelly. Spencer was pulling tacks, wishing he could rip but knowing better.

Aunt Kelly whispered to Zee Zee, "Do you think you would want to show her your house? To keep her occupied a little longer?"

Zee Zee didn't. She didn't want to share her house with Aunt Vivian any more than she did her summer. But then that little twinge of shame nipped at her again. Perhaps she could. "But she can't climb the ladder," she said.

"She can if she wants to," said Aunt Kelly. "She can if she's asked."

Spencer had most of the back off the couch now, and was feeling around inside. There were footsteps in the hall again. Zee Zee ran for the stairs.

If Zee Zee was surprised at Aunt Vivian, Aunt Vivian was more surprised at herself. When she had been asked to climb the ladder, she had done it. She found Zee Zee's attic room charming, though she did not say so.

But it was the little house that made Aunt Vivian behave as none of them had expected.

At first she only sniffed. From the outside the house seemed nothing more than a rectangular box, for it had been made to fit snugly between other houses. But then Aunt Vivian saw the frosted glass front, the tall windows divided with plain mahogany strips, the little tiled entrance, and the carved door.

She looked inside. The light shone down through the glass roof, making the garden bright. A red tapestry hung on one wall. Small benches were covered with bright pillows. Little mosaic pots stood about, ready to be planted.

Rooms with balconies faced the garden. And in the balcony railing were tiny carved animals and birds.

"Oh," said Aunt Vivian, bending down to see better, "those tiny carved animals!" She was remembering something long forgotten.

It was a snowy Christmas morning. The tree was bright with ornaments, the sun just peeping in at it. Two small children, a boy and a girl, crept down the squeaky wooden stairs, hand in hand. Under the towering tree was a whole procession of tiny wooden animals, bright and new, prancing gaily. There were cows and bears and monkeys, chickens, birds, and a giraffe. How long ago, how forgotten, that Christmas had been.

Aunt Vivian sat down beside the table. She looked again

at the little animals and pictured a small child peering over the railings. She began to think herself small, so she could go inside.

Zee Zee was quiet. Aunt Vivian put a finger in, to touch the little cushions. She looked in at the library, the fireplace, not yet finished, the bookshelves waiting for books. Why, sitting there and looking into the patio, one would never think one was in a city apartment. How lovely it was.

Aunt Vivian did not know quite what to say. She was not used to complimenting people. Especially children. Maybe, thought Aunt Vivian suddenly, I have never thought of children as people before. "I wish," she said finally, "that I might give this little house a present." It sounded stiff, awkward, she thought. Would Zee Zee take offense?

She did not. "I should like that," said Zee Zee. "I should like that very much."

"Well, I thought," continued Aunt Vivian, "that perhaps a little tree . . ." She hesitated, waiting for Zee Zee.

"It would be a lovely present," said Zee Zee. "I would take very kind care of it."

Later she was to say, "Why, Mother, she really liked my house! She was a little girl once, too. How long ago it must have been!"

Aunt Kelly, reaching into the dark interior of the couch, drew her hand back suddenly. "He's there, all right," she said. Spencer looked at her with admiration. He reached in. Finally he withdrew his hand, the snake held behind the head, and coiled around his arm, hissing.

When Aunt Vivian and Zee Zee came down, the couch was back in place, Spencer had disappeared, and all was serene.

"Where is it?" Mother asked him sternly when Aunt Vivian had gone.

"In my room," said Spence. "He bit Aunt Kelly."

"It's only a garter snake," said Aunt Kelly.

Mother had more to say to Spencer, but it was said in private.

Chapter 16

Buttons was even saucier after his night out. Mel's wet tears on his neck hadn't been noticed (Mel thought), and he was his same old sassy self again.

It was Mel's habit, when the day had been long and hot, and she was feeling sleepy, to throw one leg over the pommel and ride sidesaddle, drowsing, letting Buttons meander sleepily through the late afternoon.

This afternoon bees buzzed and squirrels scolded lazily. Ducks drowsed and birds sounded fuzzy.

Mel's head nodded. Buttons's head, too. But his ears wiggled menacingly, if only Mel had been awake enough to see. On they wandered, horse and girl. From the meadow where she was gathering stones, Zee Zee watched them, laughing.

Sleepy, sleepy, nodding Mel. Sleepy Buttons, thought Mel.

Before she knew what had happened Mel was standing on the ground; Buttons had turned and was facing away from her, pulling. Then the reins were out of her hands and he was galloping, head up, reins dragging dangerously, up the trail toward home.

There stood Melani on the trail, still half asleep.

She started to run after him, as fast as she could go. She thought of the night he had been loose, and she ran faster, shouting. Zee Zee was running, too.

Down the trail came a group of riders, people with proper coats and boots, two by two, snaffle bits and running martingales polished. Mel's face turned pink—a dirty, disheveled little girl in blue denims, chasing her fat, roach-maned pony, reins flying.

One of the riders made a grab for the reins. Buttons whirled, and was galloping back down the trail, toward Mel.

He swerved into a patch of brush, Mel after him and Zee Zee close behind. "I've got him, I've got him," shouted Mel. The riders went on their way, laughing. But she didn't have him. He had disappeared.

Through the brush they pushed, Zee Zee here and Mel there. No sign of Buttons. On through the brush they went, hair getting full of twigs, hands scratched, neither caring. They could hear nothing but themselves, no matter how they listened.

Mel got clear through the thicket first, to the edge of the hill. She turned to go along it, putting out her hand to push a branch aside. There was a great wisp of horsehair on it. She looked all around. Right in front of her, staring darkly, was an opening into the hill. She went through it, calling softly for Zee Zee.

It was dark inside but not black. She stood a minute to get her bearings and waited for Zee Zee to catch up.

Hand in hand they went into the gloom, into a dim cave, but not a cave, for through an opening at the top they could see sky and trees.

Ahead, brown eyes watched them. Ears twitched. Tail switched. A dark form turned and galloped off, right under their noses.

They ran, one at either side, the cave getting lighter. As they got near the center and paused for breath they could see shadows in a thicket, one moving. Mel walked ahead, softly, toward it. The shadow waited for her, still dragging reins. As she got almost to it, inches from the reins, the shadow ran madly, ears back.

Melani said a very bad word.

The two girls drew together, whispering. How could they ever catch him?

Meanwhile, Buttons had stepped on his reins. Now was their chance, if they only knew it. But a minute later he had jerked his head and broken them. Off he went, galloping, bucking across the little field in which he found himself.

"Grain," said Mel, "if we only had some grain."

"Shall I go and get some?" asked Zee Zee.

"Someone would see you and know I let him get loose," said Mel, ashamed.

"Oats?" asked Zee Zee. "Oats from the kitchen? Rolled oats?"

"Yes," said Mel. "In a coffee can. Hurry."

Zee Zee did. She hurried as fast as she could. Jeffy would have returned with her, but remembering how he had gone astray the last time, she shut him in the kitchen.

Mel stood by the entrance, waiting, peering into the dimness. I wonder, she thought, if he can get out another way. She strained her eyes to see. The place was rather like a cave and rather like a valley, dark at this end, lighter at the other, cliffs all around and not much sky, only one small patch, laced with trees. Buttons had disappeared, but she could hear him rustling, and she could hear a stream splashing somewhere ahead of her.

When Zee Zee returned she guarded the entrance while Mel advanced, quietly, seeming unconcerned, meandering, watching the ground. It would never do to appear to be looking for someone. She scuffed her feet and peered up beneath her lashes. Then she saw him standing in the shadows, directly ahead, quietly watching her. She shook her can of grain carelessly, making a lovely shooshing noise, all unintentional.

She strolled. She dawdled. She stopped and yawned. She happened to shake the grain, accidentally.

The shadow drew closer, ears up, nose twitching.

She stood, grain held out, shooshing.

A warm nose thrust into the coffee can. She grabbed the reins.

But horsehair reins, not leather, lay scratchily in her palm; a pale, dappled nose snuffled grain. A delicate white

body stood before her, slim legs, long pasterns, delicately arched neck. The stallion was warm and solid when she touched him.

"It's the ghost," whispered Mel, "but he's real!" The grain was gone and the stallion was beginning to look around, troubled.

She peered into the gloom. Ahead of her, in a thicket, shapes were moving, one four-legged and fat. Other horses moved beside it. Smaller figures, too. Dogs? No, colts. And another figure, human. Holding Buttons. Mel turned the stallion and led him toward the figure.

Zee Zee stood at the entrance, watching.

Chapter 17

The boy was not much older than Zee Zee, but much taller. He had dark brown eyes, almost black, a thin face and build, and his hands were brown and strong. The stallion snuffled and nuzzled his neck and the colts pushed their noses into his hands trustingly. The mares regarded him with limpid brown eyes. There were three mares and three colts, very little ones. "Born this spring," said Will.

"But how . . . ?" Zee Zee began.

Will had given Buttons back to Mel and had drawn a great gate covered with vines over the cave entrance. Now they sat on a flat rock, the horses grazing nearby, and Zee Zee wishing she had brought enough grain for all.

Will looked at them both, wondering, measuring. Can I trust them? he was thinking. Would they tell my secret? Would they? He thought not.

"We won't tell," whispered Mel, enchanted.

"Please," said Zee Zee. "We won't tell. We have seen him before."

Startled, Will's dark eyes were very intense.

"Not here," said Mel quickly, seeing his fright. "I saw him standing on a hill in the fog, then Zee Zee saw him when Buttons got loose. It was you who caught Buttons, wasn't it?"

"Yes," said Will, "it was."

Then Will told them how he had watched Buttons lead the riders through the valley, always just ahead of them, and how, standing in the fog and shadows, he had roped Buttons and snubbed him to a tree, then ridden off into the night, the stallion nervous at the approach of riders.

"But however did they get here?" asked Zee Zee. "Were they wild horses? Where did they come from?" The girls couldn't contain themselves, watching the delicate mares, the tiny colts, almost as strange and wild as antelopes, grazing in the cave valley.

Will looked closely at the girls. They knew his secret— he might as well tell the rest of the story.

And so, as Will talked, the girls began to see before them, as clearly as a picture, the place where Will and the horses had come from. Thick green grass, knee-deep, waved in long ripples like the sea; fields heavy with sweet-smelling alfalfa lay ready to be harvested; yellow sheafs of hay stood in neat rows. Great stands of eucalyptus trees bordered a wide stream, and weathered gray houses and barns, strongly built and sun-soaked, stood clustered around the ranch yard. Arabian horses grazed and galloped in the pastures, a silver colt among them, and purebred cattle dotted the hills.

In one of the little one-room houses beside the great house a tall man, dark of hair and eye, and a small, thin boy cooked their meals and washed their clothes and went to sleep as early as the sun, rising before it to go to the fields and the barns and the pastures.

For the little boy there were eggs to gather, cows to milk, and harder and longer tasks as he grew older. But always joyful tasks: baby ducks and chickens to care for, colts to see to, and as he grew older, more and more there was the companionship of tasks shared. "You are getting to be a fine horseman," the father said once, just before he went away. "Mr. Stebens says you can do my job while I'm in the Army." Will was then twelve years old.

The little house felt empty after his father had gone, and Will spent more and more time with the horses. In the evenings, after his regular chores, he would put halters on the colts and gentle them. "They will be no problem at all to break, after so much gentling," said Mr. Stebens. And they were not. The young silver stallion took to the bridle and saddle with never a buck, never a wiggle of protest, ears up and neck arched, ready for adventure. "Ankar, Ankar," Will would say, giving him carrot tops, "you are the finest of all." The stallion would greet Will joyfully every morning, as bright as the sun and twice as welcome.

Then Will's father was killed. There was only a telegram

to tell him, and Mr. Stebens to say it was true, though Will could not believe it. In his loneliness he turned more and more to Ankar and the other horses.

"You have no one now," said Mr. Stebens, "no one to provide for you but your own self. Maybe this will help," and he handed Will a long brown envelope. They were sitting in Mr. Stebens's study, a place where Will seldom went. What could Mr. Stebens be giving him? Will opened the envelope.

At first he didn't understand. He knew what the papers were, but he didn't understand. The first one had Ankar's name, and gave the stallion's breeding lines. Will knew they were Ankar's registration papers. But what had this to do with Will? He sat dumbly for a minute.

There were three more papers. One was for the yearling filly Shelastra, whom he had just started to break; one for the three-year-old mare Tickalong, on whom he worked cattle, and the last paper was for Night Princess, a lovely bay filly.

"They are your horses, now, Will," said Mr. Stebens. Will could not find a voice to thank Mr. Stebens. He ran from the room, chagrined at his own clumsiness. Then he went back, stammering, to apologize. Mr. Stebens did a rare thing. He put his arm around Will, not at all man to man as he usually treated him, but more as Will's father might have done.

Finally, Will believed it. "They are yours now," said Mr. Stebens again. "You may pay for their board by breeding Ankar to my mares, at the usual rate. We will figure it all out and put it down on paper." And that is what they did.

Tickalong had been bred months before and was already growing heavy. Will was as proud as a grandfather waiting for his first grandchild.

"I had the papers all ready to send in, to make the transfer of ownership," Will said. "They were on my table, waiting for someone to go to town with the mail. That was the night it happened."

Visions of horror rose before the girls as Will described waking that night, the windows dancing with queer red light, and running to the stable where flames leaped from the roof and horses screamed in terror.

A violent wind whipped the smoke into his nostrils, and the flames leaped into the air, carrying smoldering pieces of shingle with them. Soon the big main house was on fire too. Will was in the stable when he saw it flare up. He paused, cruelly torn between fear for Mr. Stebens and fear for the horses. "Go on, go on," shouted a voice behind him, "I'm all right," and Mr. Stebens caught up with him, bringing towels to cover the horses' eyes. They led them out, two at a time. They had Ankar out, rearing and screaming with the pain, before the first timber fell. One small yearling was caught beneath it. Mr. Stebens grabbed the timber in his own arms, lifting it as best he could until Will could reach him to give help.

"The yearling was too badly burned, and had to be shot," said Will. "Three horses were lost. We got the rest out. Ankar and Shelastra have scars. Tickalong and Night Princess were out to pasture."

By the time the horses were safe there was nothing left of the ranch. Nothing at all. Even the fences were charred timbers lying on the ground in the ranch yard, and the houses of the ranch hands were heaps of black, smoking rubble. The firemen, when they arrived, managed to save the pastures; the mares and colts huddled, trembling, at the far corners, leaping fences, some of them, or breaking through the fences in a panic.

It took a week to find the mares and colts who had got out, and to mend the fences and start to clean up the ruins.

Three days later, in the hospital, Mr. Stebens was dead.

Then came the lawyers, and the heirs, arriving almost at once. The registration papers had been burned, the transfers unrecorded. Tickalong was heavy in foal. The lawyers had a man in to take stock of the horses. "They will all be sold. Everything must go," said the lawyers. "The land will be divided among the heirs."

Will was terrified. What proof did he have that the four horses were his? No one would believe him.

That night, with the help of one of the ranch hands, Will loaded Ankar and the mare and fillies into a van and drove quietly north along the coast. "I know a place no one knows," said young John Elson, who was driving. "No one will ever find it."

"Is there pasture?" asked Will.

"A little," said John, "but not very good. It's too dark." He told Will about the cave valley. "You will have to buy feed," said John. "It would be better if you could work at another ranch, and board the horses there."

"I wouldn't dare," said Will. "They would find me."

"Yes," said John, "but you'll have to get a job somewhere. My uncle has a grocery near this place. It's not big, but we can try."

By dawn they had the horses unloaded and settled, and a gate built and covered with green branches.

The uncle did need help. It was a small market, but big enough to need Will, and the uncle did not ask questions. He liked Will, and he thought that whatever strange thing he was up to—so young a boy, working so hard, going off

into the dusk after work without a word about a family—
it was not a bad thing, and he let well enough alone.

The summer that Tickalong's first colt was born, Will
was up all one night, in the full of the moon, helping her.
At dawn a little chestnut filly stood before him, wobbly
and big-eyed and golden as the morning.

"She was a picture," said Will. "I didn't have papers,
and I hated to sell her, but I had to. I wanted to set a little
aside. Some day someone will find this place"—and here he
paused and looked at the girls—"and if they take the horses
from me, I want something to start again with." He looked
resigned, and Zee Zee thought how very hard it was for
him. I wonder, she thought, if I could ever have done it.

"But couldn't you prove, somehow . . . ?" Mel began.

"How?" asked Will, and shook his head.

It was growing darker in the valley. The girls knew they
would be missed. "Please," said Zee Zee, "you'll let us
come back? You will if we're careful, won't you?"

"Yes," said Will, though he looked wary, "but only in
the fog, or the dark."

Chapter 18

Fall was edging closer; fall, and school. "Don't think of it," said Zee Zee. They tried not to.

At the end of July there was a very warm spell, following a week of fog in which Mel and Zee Zee went every morning to see Will and Ankar and the mares and colts. They never took poor Jeffy, who had to be shut in the house. "He would be a dead giveaway," said Will, "if he ever came here alone and asked to be let in." He was right, of course, but it was growing harder to find excuses to lock Jeffy in at home.

"We must think of something," said Zee Zee.

"But what?" said Mel.

"Let's ask Will," said Zee Zee.

"All right," said Mel, yawning. It was a long day for Mel, hurrying to the cave at dawn, then home for break-

fast and back to the stables. She was learning to halter-
break the colts and teach them to lead, and Zee Zee was
learning to ride a little, though the fat mares, concerned
with their colts and led by Will, were not much of a challenge.

Finally, Will let Zee Zee ride alone, riding by her side. He was teaching her to use the hackamore. "It's different from a bridle," said Zee Zee, having watched Mel.

"Yes," said Will, showing her how the little block under the chin worked in place of a bit, and why there should be a tiny jerk instead of a gentle pull to tell the horse what you wanted. "Like this," he would say, and Zee Zee would feel the mare respond easily. His brown hand over hers was very warm. The colt galloped at their side, bucking and kicking, and sometimes wanting lunch, so that they finally had to stop and let him drink.

"Will you sell all the colts?" asked Zee Zee.

"I think so," said Will sadly. "But maybe not all," he said, looking at the stud colt. "Maybe not all."

"Ask him now," said Mel the next morning. "Ask him if we can tell Mother."

"All right," said Zee Zee. And she did.

Finally Will agreed. "But no one else," he said.

"We promise," said the girls solemnly.

And so they told Mother about the cave. They told her the whole story, every bit. "You might as well," Will had said. "Half a story is no good."

Mother listened quietly, curled up in a chair in the studio. "I'll keep Jeffy in," she said. "What a sad story it is. Poor Will. It must be very hard, keeping them hidden. A very hard life for a boy."

They didn't see Will again for a week. The weather turned hot and sunny, and the park was so crowded with summer people that Will could only slip out of the cave before dawn and back again after dark. It worried him to be gone so long.

But the next week turned foggy again. The girls were there early, before five, wrapped warm, chewing cold biscuits and ham. They had brought some for Will. ("I don't think he gets enough to eat," Mel had said. "He buys feed with his pay," Zee Zee had replied, thinking how thin Will looked.)

"Mel is getting the colts nicely broke," said Will, sitting on a rock eating biscuits, "and all by herself, too. She has learned very fast." It was true, she had. The colts would lead nicely now, encouraged often with a pat or a rub behind the ears. Only when they got hungry did they balk.

"How can you sell them?" asked Zee Zee. "Won't people ask where they came from?"

"Yes," said Will, ashamed. "I don't like having to lie, and it's not right to sell them without papers, but there's nothing else to do." His brown eyes could be gay and dancing, as when he scolded Buttons, but Zee Zee thought she had never seen eyes that could be sadder.

I wish, thought Zee Zee, dreaming, I wish I had a brother like Will. But she didn't really. She was quite content to have Will just as he was.

"But you won't sell the stud colt," said Zee Zee, watching the gray colt run hungrily to his mother as Mel turned him loose. "What are you going to name him, Will?" Will's hands were whittling a piece of wood.

"On his papers I would put Rankashan," said Will. "I wish I could register him. But for a stable name, I think

I'll call him Little Ghost." Ankar came up to him and pushed his nose into the whittling. Will put away his knife and rubbed Ankar's ears.

"Mist Princess fits the bay filly," said Will, "and I think I'll call the chestnut filly Shazara. They really should have Arab names." He slapped Ankar on the rump, sending him running and bucking across the field. Little Ghost ran out to meet him, kicking and snorting, starting a game. They tore about madly, playing, shying around the shed where Mel was hanging up the halter.

As she closed the door of the shed, Mel glanced up at the opening at the top of the valley. A lace of trees sheltered it. Something was moving there. A shadow moved at the edge of the opening and disappeared.

"What kind of a shadow?" asked Zee Zee.

"I thought . . . I don't know," said Mel. "Could it have been a person?"

"Not likely," said Will. "It's steep and rocky up there, and the hole is well hidden."

"Could it have been a squirrel or rabbit?" Zee Zee said hopefully.

"It was too large," said Mel.

"Don't worry," said Will, patting her shoulder. "Perhaps it was a hawk, hunting in the rocks."

"I hope so," said Mel, unconvinced.

Chapter 19

Jeffy did not like being kept in. He was not used to it—
Mel dressing in her stable clothes and going off at dawn.
He was shut in Mother's bedroom, where Mother was still
asleep. From the window, paws on the sill, he watched the
children go.

He pushed his nose into Mother's pillow, nuzzling her
cheek, whining, but he got only a sleepy grumble in reply.
Then he curled up in Mother's slipper chair, head between
paws. He sighed great doggy sighs. He sighed again. He
got up and paced the room, looking out the window once
more. The children had disappeared into some trees, and
there was nothing to see. He nudged the door. It wiggled.
He dug at it with his paw. It moved. He dug some more,
pulling with his claws, nosing in as the crack grew larger.
It was opening. Out went Jeffy, into the hall.

"You didn't shut it tightly," Zee Zee said later to Mel.

"It was you who shut it," said Mel.

"No, you," said Zee Zee, angry.

"It doesn't really matter now, does it?" said Mother.

"No, but I didn't do it," cried both girls together.

Jeffy didn't pause in the hall. Down the stairs: no one in the living room. Into the kitchen: no one there either. Deb and Linda still sleeping. Kitchen door securely closed. What had Mel been thinking of, leaving him like that?

Aunt Kelly was up and about. She could hear Jeff pacing the floor above her, his nails clicking on the linoleum. She had been out; her shoes were wet and sandy.

She was disappointed at not having seen the ghost. Every morning she waited for him. She had not seen him again, but she had seen hoofprints once. Perhaps they were his. Her face was pink with the cold air, her patchy short hair awry, her eyes sparkling. She badly wanted her coffee. The water was hot, but when she opened the can there was no coffee there.

"Darn," said Aunt Kelly, "I forgot." Taking a key, she went up the back stairs, the empty can in her hand.

Jeffy nosed her hand and pushed against her side. He pushed her back toward the door, whining.

"What are you doing by yourself?" Aunt Kelly asked him. "Mel's not still in bed?" He whined again, nosing her once more toward the door. "But she wouldn't shut you in," said Aunt Kelly, seeing the milk left out and crumbs on the table, ham scraps and a dirty knife on the board. "She wouldn't leave you!" said Aunt Kelly indignantly, seeing Mel had done just that. "Zee Zee, too, I guess," continued Aunt Kelly, whispering. There were two chalky milk glasses, side by side. "What are those two up to, that you can't see?" asked Aunt Kelly, taking Jeffy's head between her hands and looking into his brown eyes. "But maybe you need to go out!" She was getting angry at careless Mel and Zee Zee. Thoughtless girls.

Coffee forgotten (though her tongue still missed the taste of it), Aunt Kelly found Jeffy's seldom used leash hanging by the broom.

She had meant to keep him in the yard, but he wouldn't have it. "All right," said Aunt Kelly, thinking again of the coffee, "all right, Jeffy, all right." He took her into the park, into the trees. He took her through bushes and tall, boggy grass. Her shoes squished. Finally she sat down on a rock, looking queerly at Jeffy, wanting her coffee, but more curious than hungry. "Jeffy, what on earth are you up to?" Jeffy looked innocent but eager.

She sat a minute, Jeff pulling toward a rocky hill ahead. "All right," she said finally, "all right, let's go see."

No one will ever know why Jeffy went to the top of the cave, and not to the entrance; no one will ever know how he found it. Perhaps the voices funneled up to his ears. But soon he had Aunt Kelly climbing rock and pushing through bushes.

She didn't see the tree-covered opening until it was right in front of her. At first it seemed to be nothing but a shallow cave, but when she got inside a great hole gaped before her.

Looking down, Aunt Kelly saw a little grassy valley, dimly lighted, and a few stunted trees. As her eyes became more used to the light, she could see animal shapes. She thought at first they were antelope or deer. "Why, they're horses," said Aunt Kelly, almost aloud. Three mares and two colts grazed beside the trees. One mare put up her ears and nickered. A third colt ran to her side, nuzzling hungrily.

Aunt Kelly lay down flat on her stomach on top of the rock, watching the scene below. Jeff whined by her side, but she hushed him, holding him short.

One of the colts was gray. Like the ghost, thought Aunt Kelly. And like the ghost he was, for one minute later the ghost himself came into view, side-stepping, snorting, wanting to play. The gray colt dashed out and a fine game started. Children would have called it a game of tag. They chased each other first one way and then another, dodging around something shadowy. A rock? "Why, it's a little shed," said Aunt Kelly. It was then that she saw Mel, hanging up the halter. She drew back off the rock just as Mel looked up.

When she peeked again, Mel was gone. "We had better go home," said Aunt Kelly to Jeff. "I have a feeling we have been prying where we do not belong."

They went home the long way, slowly, Aunt Kelly thinking about what she had seen. So the ghost had been a real horse, after all. This disappointed her; she rather wished he had been a ghost for sure. But no matter, he was beautiful, and still a mystery.

From the back step she could hear voices raised. She knew now that Jeff had been shut in for a reason. She felt ashamed, but she might as well face the girls. Voices were rising again. "But I didn't," came Mel's wail through the door.

I can't just stand here, thought Aunt Kelly finally. She opened the door, and the noisy kitchen was suddenly silent. Everyone was there, even Spence, looking at Aunt Kelly and Jeffy. Spence broke the silence, pointing: "You see, there he is, with Aunt Kelly. Where would he go if he had gotten out?" Spence scratched his head. "Why all the hassle, anyway? Girls!" he finished eloquently.

"We went for a walk," said Aunt Kelly lamely. "On the leash," she continued. "Jeffy, that is. I would love some coffee. We didn't get into any trouble," said Aunt Kelly, looking at Mel. "We just took a walk. I found Jeffy in the kitchen. He wanted out. I was afraid to let him loose. His feet are wet." It was hard to stop talking, everyone was so silent. She bent to take off Jeffy's leash. "It was a very dull walk," said Aunt Kelly, looking again at Mel. Mother was pouring coffee and buttering toast.

Chapter 20

When they were alone Zee Zee said to Mel, "Do you think she saw?"

"Yes," said Mel, "but she won't tell. Why can't we talk to her? I know she saw."

"Let's ask Mother," said Zee Zee.

"You must ask Will first," said Mother.

Zee Zee went that night to ask. It had fogged in early, and while Mel was still at the stables Zee Zee slipped through the gate to the cave, closing it behind her.

Will was not there, but there was a stack of bulging gunny sacks near the gate. "Alfalfa and molasses," said Zee Zee, smelling them.

A minute later the gate opened and Will slipped inside, another bag over his shoulder. It must weigh a hundred pounds, thought Zee Zee.

"How long have you been here?" asked Will.

"Just," said Zee Zee. "I have something to tell you."

Will slung the bag down with the others and sat on top of it. He made Zee Zee feel shy and nervous, sitting there quietly, waiting for her to speak. She wished there were not so many people minding Will's business. It's all our fault, thought Zee Zee. If we had never come here . . . well, it's Buttons's fault, too, I guess.

"What is it?" said Will evenly, waiting.

"Don't look like that," said Zee Zee. "It's nothing bad," and she told him.

"You're not sure she knows," said Will when she had finished.

"No," said Zee Zee, "but Mel thinks so."

"And if she did, could you trust her?" asked Will.

"Oh, yes," said Zee Zee, "absolutely you could." Zee Zee was close to tears; Will was so quiet, so solemn. What if she and Mel were responsible for getting him found out? "We will be more careful," said Zee Zee, "but please, let us come back." She felt strange and shy without Melani—it had always been the three of them.

Will looked down at her gently. He put his arm around her shoulder. "You'll be late for dinner, Zee Zee. Everything will be all right. Come back after dinner if you can. We'll take Ankar out. But we'll stay off the hills." Will laughed.

He didn't say yes or no about Aunt Kelly.

"All right," said Mother, "for a little while. But stay with Will. I don't like you out at night alone. Get Will to walk you home. You could say he was from school if anyone saw you." The girls' eyes shone.

"We'll bring Will home with us, to tell Aunt Kelly himself," said Zee Zee, inspired. "Then he can see what she's like."

"Will he come, do you think?" said Mel.

"I don't know," said Zee Zee. "Maybe he will. Maybe."

"We'll make him come," said Mel.

"Not Will," said Zee Zee, "not unless he wants to." She hoped he'd want to.

The night was like a story. It was silver and black velvet, tall grass white in the moonlight, fog rolling in patches, one minute like a white curtain, the next minute gone. They did not take Ankar far, but Will, finding a clear patch of field, galloped him and worked him, sliding, turning, backing, the girls sitting close together, watching.

They had never seen anything more beautiful. Will hardly touched the reins and Ankar turned so quickly that Will's boot brushed the grass. He did figure-eights with the reins just moving on his neck, sliding to a stop with his chin tucked nicely down. He could whirl to right and left so fast he looked almost magic; he would run backward at merely a touch of the reins.

"He's so lovely," whispered Mel. "He doesn't seem real, he's so lovely."

"He still looks like a ghost horse," said Zee Zee, and he did, like a dancing white ghost there in the silver meadow, like a fairy horse whirling to some unheard music.

Will didn't want to go to see Aunt Kelly. He said he would take the girls home, but he wouldn't come in.

"It's only Aunt Kelly," whispered Mel, taking his hand. "You'll like her."

"But what good will it do," asked Will, "to have one more know? What good?"

Nevertheless he came.

There was a fire burning in her living room; they could see the smoke from the chimney rising into the fog. Aunt Kelly was typing—they could hear the typewriter as they crowded onto the porch. Zee Zee knocked quickly, before Will could change his mind. "You'll see," whispered Mel, squeezing his hand, "you'll like her."

The room was warm and cozy, the fire bright, the curtains pulled, the lamps making yellow pools on the desk and on the red table in the kitchen. Aunt Kelly poured milk into a pan for cocoa and set the girls to making sandwiches.

"You've been out in the fog," said Aunt Kelly, settling Will by the fire. Will had never seen so many books as lined the fireplace. "It's beautiful out," said Aunt Kelly. Will looked startled. "I was out earlier," she said easily, "just as the moon started to rise." That had been hours ago. Will relaxed. "I was looking for my ghost," said Aunt Kelly. Will looked uneasy again. "But I did not see him. I doubt I'll ever see him again," said Aunt Kelly. "I've waited so many times."

Will knew he should say something like, "A ghost? A real ghost?" or, "Was it a howling, wicked ghost?" but he could say nothing; he could not be light about it. Was Aunt Kelly being cruel, or only talking to make conversation? No, he knew better than that. Perhaps teasing him?

"He is the white ghost of the sea," continued Aunt Kelly, unabashed. "At least, I saw him by the sea, as if he had come from it. He is silvery-white, and the most beautiful thing I have ever seen, like a vision, like a fairy horse; and fast as the wind."

Will was softened, won. He could see it in Aunt Kelly's eyes; teasing him or not, she was telling the truth. She had thought Ankar the most beautiful thing in the world. "Do you think he is?" whispered Will in spite of himself, leaning forward in his chair. There was something about Aunt Kelly which made him trust her, something of Mel about her, something like a child or an animal.

Zee Zee came up beside his chair and sat down on the arm of it, but she said nothing.

"Yes, I do," said Aunt Kelly simply. "I have gone to the beach every morning to look for him. He was like a dream. I should like more than anything to see him again."

"Would you?" asked Will. "Would you really like to see him again? Even if you might be disappointed?"

Now it was Aunt Kelly's turn to wonder what to say. Half a truth is a lie, and she knew she could not lie to this boy. "I wouldn't be disappointed," said Aunt Kelly. "I think I really know he is not a ghost; though I like to pretend. I saw him once in the valley; I know he must be real. But to me he is a magic horse." Zee Zee could have hugged Aunt Kelly.

Then the story was out; Aunt Kelly confessed. It was hard to do. She felt an intruder. But still her instinct led her on. Somehow Will was anxious to tell her the rest, anxious to share with her, and not leave her wondering— she seemed so eager, yet so afraid of intruding.

So he told about the ranch, about growing up there, about the horses, the telegram, the night in Mr. Stebens's study, about the fire, and all that happened after it. Zee Zee and Mel sat quietly, seeing it all again, feeling all that Will had felt. Then they told their parts of the story, interrupting each other, eager, breathless. Will smiled quietly as they went on, bright-eyed, falling over each other's words.

"And the papers were all burned?" said Aunt Kelly, coming back to Will. "And there was nothing else to show that you owned them? The lawyers didn't know?"

Will shook his head.

"And Mr. Stebens, did you say his first name was Robert?" Will nodded. "Mr. Stebens had told no one else?"

"No," said Will, "no one. No one I know of."

Will walked home in the fog, slipping quietly in at the gate. He washed in the little stream and unrolled his bed-roll beside the wall of the shed. Ankar came and nosed at his face, nickering softly. The moon shone down through the wisps of fog, making Ankar look truly a ghost in its pale light. Will sighed. Somehow he felt warm and snug and relieved, as if a great weight had been lifted from his shoulders. She will never tell, thought Will. Somehow, it's nice. It's nice to have her know.

Chapter 21

Mel was talking to Mr. Blake. Rather, she was sitting in the tack room reading something while Mr. Blake sat across from her at a small desk, writing.

As she read, Mel's eyes got bigger and bigger. Her mouth was making a round o. "You'll catch flies," said Mr. Blake. Mel shut her mouth. "What do you think?" asked Mr. Blake.

"Think!" said Mel. "Of course she'll let me. She must!"

"Must she?"

"Oh, yes," said Mel. "Oh, yes. How many classes? How many days? When would we go?" There were a thousand questions.

"It's a two-day show," said Mr. Blake. "We would leave on Friday, a week, come home on Monday morning. There is a motel nearby where the show people stay." He paused, drinking coffee.

"Oh, dear," said Mel, thinking of the expense. What if Mother *could* not let her go? There were the lessons, after all.

Mr. Blake, watching her, knew what she was thinking. "Your mother made the reservations last night," he said.

Mel beamed, and bounced up and down in her chair. "Show me again," she said, handing Mr. Blake the class list and scooting up beside him.

"Well, here," said Mr. Blake, "are the children's classes. Here, Seat and Hands, English, and Children's Hunters. Rambler will be fine for both of these."

"Hunters?" Mel said, breathless. "I'm to ride him in the Hunters?"

"Of course," said Mr. Blake. "Children's Hunters. The jumps aren't so high as in jumper classes—it's way-of-going that counts."

"Yes," said Mel.

"Here is Children's Western Trail Horse, and Seat and Hands, Western. One of the boarders, Mr. Jonathan, has a new Western pony. He would like you to ride for him. That is, if you would like to," said Mr. Blake.

"Do you think I can?" asked Mel.

"If I didn't think so," said Mr. Blake, "I wouldn't bother with it."

The little boys sat on a rock by a stream in the park. Their faces were very dirty, their hands grimy, but their feet surprisingly pale and clean, dangling bare in the icy water. There were six little boys this time. One had brought a friend. A new friend. He had a .22. He also had ammunition. Each boy's pockets bulged, suspiciously sagging and heavy. Each one licked his lips, rubbed his grimy hands together, and looked as roguish as ever a small boy looked. Two boys carried cloth bags in which to put their catch, "Just stunned," as Spence said.

It was not until the next morning that Mel thought about clothes. Waking, she sat straight up in bed, rousing Jeffy. "I have no clothes," she said aloud. "How can I go?" She thought of boots, shining, and jodhpurs, smooth and snug. Not in blue denims, thought Mel, seeing herself in the show ring, denims flapping sloppily above her tennis shoes, all the other riders properly dressed and smart. "Oh," said Mel with a wail, piling out of bed, "how can I go?"

She piled onto Mother's bed, waking her. "Mother, what about clothes?" She was getting tearful. "How can I go without clothes?"

Mother, sleepy, only mumbled. Melani shook her. Finally she woke, looking cross. Mel wondered if this had been the best time to ask.

Mother grumbled some more. "If you are going to wake me, Mel, go and get me some coffee." She frowned.

Mel did, quietly.

"Now," said Mother, cupping her hands around the coffee mug, "what did you say?"

"I said," said Mel, "how can I ride without clothes?"

"Hmmm," said Mother. "You'll need Western and English both, won't you?"

"Oh, dear," said Mel. She had forgotten the Western.

Mother set down her cup. "Do you really think I would have told Mr. Blake you could go if I had not thought about clothes?" she asked.

"No," said Mel, trustingly, eyes brighter, "but how can we?"

"We'll manage," said Mother. "First of all, the Western. Mr. Blake says you can perfectly well wear jodphur boots with Levi's. He says he can borrow a hat. That leaves a shirt to buy." Mother sipped more coffee. "And the jodhpur boots, of course. Then jodhpurs, and a coat for the hunting class. A plain white blouse will do, and you'll not need a hat." Mother giggled. "Mr. Blake will lend you a tie. You can tuck it in your belt."

"A man's tie?"

"Of course," said Mother. "Come on, get dressed if you are going shopping with me."

Zee Zee was digging earth in the garden. She didn't need much, but it had to be good. Aunt Vivian had brought the trees. Not one, but six. They were bonsai, dwarf pepper trees, and lemon, three of each. "The lemons will bear," said Aunt Vivian. "Look!" There were tiny blossoms on them.

Aunt Vivian had shown her how to transplant the little trees. "You must do this every so often," said Aunt Vivian, "and trim the roots, so, or they will become root-bound and die." She showed Zee Zee how to trim off extra growth from the top, too. They were the most marvelous little trees. Zee Zee had known she wanted live ones, but she had not really known how cunning they would be. Cunning, yes, that was Aunt Vivian's word. It seemed to fit just right.

The saddle shop was grand. It smelled of leather and saddle soap. There were new pale leather saddles on racks, bridles and bits hanging above them, hackamores, even hair ones like Will's; there were rawhide nosebands, stud chains, colt halters, lunge lines; there were English saddles and Western, racing saddles, yellow saddle pads and red-and-black Western saddle blankets. There were boots and shirts and chaps, even fur ones; derbies; plaid blankets, plain blankets with initials; buckets, spurs, blanket bars, brushes,

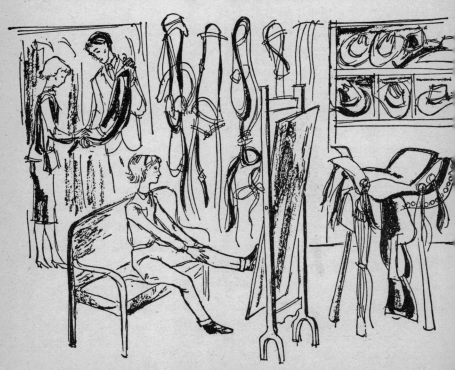

curry combs—everything Mel could possibly imagine, and more things she couldn't.

"Elastic cinches?" said Mel. "Steel hackamores?" She had never heard of such things. There were quarter boots, wraps, hobbles, and even a life-size store model of a lady dressed in a pink hunting coat, on a life-size horse, in the store window.

First Mel was fitted for boots. "Try black," said the salesman. "I think I have a buy in a coat that will fit." He disappeared, returning in a minute with a tweedy black wool hunting coat. Split tails, long waist, three-button front, a brass ring sewn into the inside of the collar. "To hang it on the tack-room door," said the salesman. "It was made for a young lady who outgrew it before she ever wore it. We can let you have it for less than the ready-made coats. Mr. Blake called me," he confided. "He is a good friend of mine."

The boots were black and shiny, the jodhpurs good beige whipcord. "Here is a little knit tie that will fit," said the salesman. "We'll throw that in for good measure." There was a Western shirt to get, blue-and-white plaid with white pearl buttons and white piping.

"I feel like a queen," whispered Mel as they left the store. "Won't Buttons be surprised? I wonder if he'll know me." Then it occurred to Mel that Buttons wasn't going. She had made a picture in her mind of Buttons, groomed and shining, with her in her black coat and black boots, her light jodhpurs and white skirt, black tie and black ribbon binding her hair. It looked grand. Buttons looked grand. She couldn't even picture herself on Rambler in the new clothes—it kept on being Buttons. Unexpectedly, a tear slid down Mel's nose.

"He won't care," said Mother, patting Mel's knee. "He wouldn't like all the fuss."

"Yes, he would," said Mel angrily.

Mr. Blake was to say, "He would like it too much. He would find some way to make trouble." Mr. Blake knew Buttons too well.

Thinking of Buttons, Mel almost didn't see Aunt Kelly get off the bus across the street—almost didn't. But she had sharp eyes, even teary. "Why didn't she ride to town with us?" said Mel, indignant.

"Perhaps it wasn't Aunt Kelly," said Mother. "Are you sure?"

"Yes," said Mel, "it was Aunt Kelly, all right." She had gone into a tall, dark-fronted building. "Aunt Kelly, Aunt Kelly," called Mel, but Aunt Kelly didn't hear. "Shall we wait?" asked Mel.

"We'd better not," said Mother. "My parking time is up. It's not long on the bus. Maybe she has other things to do."

Chapter 22

Mel was practicing. She jumped Rambler every day, went through the equitation drills, then rode the Western pony James at a slow lope, a jog, stirrups longer than on Rambler, reins in one hand, loose, opening gates, stepping carefully over logs. "She does well enough to put her in the Ladies'," said Mr. Jonathan. "Do we still have time to enter her?"

"Yes," said Mr. Blake, "we do."

Mel still felt bad about Buttons. "Couldn't we enter him in something?" she asked Mr. Blake. She was sure Buttons knew; she felt unfaithful. "Buttons is not a hunter," Mr. Blake said. "Rambler can be in both classes, and there is no room in the van for Buttons. We are taking other boarders besides James, you know." Mel knew he was right, but it made her feel no better. She wanted to wear her new clothes on Buttons; she wanted him to look smart and as well got up as Rambler.

"I will wear them on Buttons first," said Mel. She did not say it to anyone but herself. It would look silly to appear at the stables in her show clothes. No one would understand, not even Mr. Blake.

Zee Zee would help her. "You hold him," said Mel, meeting Zee Zee in the park. "Hold him close, don't let him turn on you. Did you bring the camera?"

"Yes," said Zee Zee.

"Then hold him, now, while I go change. I won't be long." And Mel dashed off for home.

Zee Zee held Buttons close as she was told, right hand grasping all four reins tightly just below the bit, left hand holding them farther down. She walked him about a little to keep him from fussing. He wanted to graze. "Not in the bit," Mel had said. "It's bad manners." Buttons glared.

Hurry up, Mel, thought Zee Zee. She did not altogether trust Buttons.

The grass was very green—succulent.

Buttons was growing angry. This little girl was not Melani. She was nobody. And she was unsure of herself. Buttons knew quite well about children like that. "Dudes," Mr. Blake would have said. Buttons knew how to handle them.

Buttons gave Zee Zee a sideways glance, appraising her. She was standing just right, facing forward. He bowed his neck, stepping up into the bit. He shifted his weight just a little. Mel would have known what he was up to. Zee Zee did not.

Whack! Buttons kicked her in the seat. She jumped around, letting go with her right hand. Then, "Ow," yowled Zee Zee. Buttons had bitten her, hard. She slapped at him. She should not have. He whirled, front feet tucked under him, as quick as a flash, and leaped away, jerking the reins from her hand. Too late she grabbed at him, nearly falling. He was halfway across the field when Mel got back. She didn't ask what happened, she just walked very slowly and quietly around the side of the field, slowly edging closer, motioning Zee Zee the other way. Buttons grazed, reins dragging, ears cocked, watching them. Slowly, slowly, Mel drew closer, Buttons watching. If it had not been for what happened next, she never would have caught him.

Buttons intended to let Mel get within a few feet of him, then leap away. He waited, pretending to be grazing. He's going to let me catch him, thought Mel. Maybe he's sorry.

Just as she reached for the reins Buttons half-reared, turning. But something hard hit his shoulder; he was knocked off balance, whirling back toward Mel. She grabbed. She had the reins. Buttons leaped past her, alarmed. A loud crash had followed the blow. Mel held on, off balance, both of them, Buttons turning almost on top of her, panicked, knocking her down. She hung on to the reins. He dragged her, but she dug in her heels obstinately. Jerking, angry, she got him stopped. She had not heard the voices and the sound of running footsteps.

"What happened?" she shouted at Zee Zee.

"I think it was a gun," said Zee Zee.

They looked at each other. Buttons was standing still

now, head down and turned a little away. Mel walked around to his off side. On his shoulder, just at the point, blood was oozing. Mel put her hand on it, then threw her arms around Buttons's neck, crying. Zee Zee pulled her away. "Let me see. My gosh, Mel, what'll we do?"

"Go for Mr. Blake," said Mel; then, "Wait. Let's see if he can walk." Crying still, she led him forward. He followed her, but it made the blood ooze more.

"It's not far," said Zee Zee.

"What will Mr. Blake say?" Mel was worried. "Oh, Zee Zee, what'll we do?"

"No matter what he says, we've got to get help," said Zee Zee. They began to lead Buttons home, slowly, Mel still crying.

"It's only a flesh wound," said Mr. Blake. "Didn't even nip the bone." He dug out the bullet with a knife, Buttons flinching. He doctored the wound. "I'll call the veterinarian for a shot, for infection," said Mr. Blake, looking at the bullet, "and call the police."

Both girls stood wide-eyed. "It could have been you, Mel," said Mr. Blake. Mel wished that it had. She put Buttons in his stall, in crossties, as she was told, to keep him from biting the dressing. There he would have to stand all night, uncomfortable, head up, not able to lie down. Melani wept again. Buttons nuzzled her neck, a thing he seldom did.

It was not until they got home that Mel, standing in front of the mirror, realized how she looked. "We'd better tell Mother," said Zee Zee.

"How can I?" wailed Mel. "It was her own clothes money, every cent. Go get Aunt Kelly, Zee Zee—maybe she can think of something."

But Aunt Kelly's apartment was locked and deserted. "She never goes out in the day," said Mel, frantic.

"Well, she's out today," said Zee Zee. Through the windows she could see that the kitchen was neat as a pin, not even a coffee cup in the sink, the bed made, the living room tidy, the fireplace cold and empty.

Linda and Deb were gone, too. "Could we sponge it ourselves?" asked Mel.

"The blood we could," said Zee Zee, "but I don't know about grass stains. And Mel, you're ripped."

"Oh, no," said Mel, biting her lip. "Oh, Mother will be livid. All right, Zee Zee, call her."

When the coat and jodhpurs came back from the cleaners three days later, the mended tear was nearly invisible. "Yes, it looks fine," Mother said. "You would never know. Come on, Mel, put them on. I will take your picture. You and Buttons." She had heard the whole story. "Then you will come home and change."

Buttons was all saddled, brushed and combed within an inch of his life, his tail braided and a red ribbon binding his forelock. Mr. Blake led him out of his stall, and waved his hat to make him put his ears up while Mother took pictures, Mel sitting straight and proud in her new clothes, Buttons looking very prim, but interested, wondering how he could turn the occasion into a more lively one. He didn't get the chance. Before he could think of an interesting idea, he was back in his stall, Mel home and sliding into her old blue denims, the riding clothes packed safely away, ready for the horse show.

"Let's say good-by to Will," said Zee Zee, the night before they were to leave.

"Let's take Aunt Kelly," cried Mel. "I think he would like us to."

"Yes," said Zee Zee, "so do I."

But when they went to get Aunt Kelly, the apartment was dark. "Come to think of it, I haven't seen her all day," said Mel.

"You don't suppose she's sick," said Mel.

"We'd know if it were that," said Zee Zee.

They slipped through the bushes and the gate and found Will sitting by a small lighted candle, mending a halter with a heavy needle and linen thread. "Did the police find out who shot Buttons?" asked Will, "or are they still looking? It makes me uneasy, having them around."

"No," said Zee Zee unhappily, "they haven't. They said they would keep watching." She felt terrible. It seemed as if she and Mel did nothing but complicate Will's life and make it even harder for him to keep the horses safe.

"It will be all right," said Will, seeing her concern. "We want whoever did it caught, that's sure."

"How could anyone?" asked Mel. "How could they?"

"Maybe it was an accident," said Will. "Maybe they were shooting at something else."

"At what?" cried both girls together. "At us, do you mean?"

"Oh, no," said Will, grinning, "but maybe squirrels, or birds."

"How awful," said Zee Zee. "I hope the police catch them."

"What if the ones with the gun find the valley?" Mel said. "Oh, they mustn't, Will. What can we do?"

"We could watch while you're at work," said Zee Zee.

"You'll be gone," said Will. "They won't come here. I promise you they won't hurt the horses. You're not to worry, either of you." He stood up and went into the little shed, returning in a minute with something which he held up to Mel, then buckled around her waist. "I thought they'd fit," said Will. "They were mine when I was little." They were Will's old chaps, scarred and molded to shape from much wearing. "You will win a class in these," said Will. "They're for luck, Mel." He patted her on the shoulder, squeezed Zee Zee's hand, and whispered "Good night" to them as they slipped through the gate.

"He really broke horses in these," said Mel, breathless. "I bet he broke Ankar in these chaps. I will win a blue ribbon for Will," she said, clasping her hands.

Chapter 23

They had reservations for two rooms, Mel and Zee Zee in one, Mother and Aunt Kelly in the other.

"But I want to go," howled Spence.

"You don't care a fig about a horse show," said Linda.

"Yes, I do," said Spence. "Yes, I do!"

"Besides, we can't afford it," said practical Deb. It was true, they could not.

"Zee Zee could stay at home," offered Spence. "She doesn't need to go. Besides, if Mother hadn't spent so much money on clothes, we could afford it."

"Hush up," said Deb finally. "You're going to stay here with us and behave."

"I won't, I won't," said Spencer, slamming out.

"I've never seen him act like this before, about something he really doesn't care about," said Linda.

"Maybe he does care," said Zee Zee.

"About horses? No, not Spence," said Deb. "He just feels left out, that's all. He's not the center of attention."

"He's making himself just that," observed Linda.

"I wonder if Mother will change her mind and let him go," said Zee Zee, hoping not. "You don't mind not going, Linda? Deb?"

"No," said Linda, "we don't mind. We have something to do at home."

"If we can keep Spence busy," said Deb.

"What is it?" asked Zee Zee.

"It's Linda's book," said Deb. "She has finished it, and I am doing the drawings. We'll have three days to work on nothing else."

"What's it about?" Zee Zee asked. "Tell me the story, Lin?"

But there wasn't time. Spencer came back into the kitchen, followed by Mother—Mother scowling, Spencer scuffing his feet.

"Spencer," said Mother, "will stay here." So it was decided, with no more fuss.

Aunt Vivian might have said, "But they are too young to stay alone."

"No," Mother would have said, "they are not."

It was nearly dark when they arrived at the fairgrounds. The horses had gone that morning. "Can't we go earlier?" Mel had pleaded.

"No," Mother had said, "I must get this work in the mail. There are no classes until tomorrow."

There was a special parking lot for trailers and vans, and for exhibitors. "That's me," said Mel, overcome; there was a sticker on the windshield which said so. There were rows and rows of stables, painted green and all alike. "How will we ever find ours?" asked Mel.

"They're numbered," said Mother. "We're twenty-six."

"Look," said Zee Zee, "the tack rooms!" Mel caught her breath. Down the rows of stalls, wherever there was a tack room, the door was open and the entrance decorated with bright cloth, top to bottom, tied back into two curtains. On the doors there were ribbons hanging in rows so thick they overlapped, rows and rows of blue ribbons, then red, then yellow, and then white. There were tack trunks and folding chairs before the doors, each in its stable's colors: red and white, orange and blue, purple and gray. Grooms and riders were soaping tack, grooming horses, sweeping, sitting talking. Even the blankets on the horses were in stable colors, some monogrammed. Everywhere there was activity. Saddle horses were having tail sets put on, taken off, manes combed, braided. Stable dogs lounged, people greeted each other boisterously.

Horses were being bedded for the night, hay carried, stalls cleaned, grain measured, water buckets filled just like at home, but here, here it was all so grand. The stable lights made everything look different, like a play on a stage.

They greeted their own horses, bedded, blanketed, and comfortable, Rambler nickering softly to Mel. James, the Western pony, had his chestnut mane and tail in braids— "To make them wavy," said Mel. He was a smart, neat pony, a small horse, really, about Buttons's size. "He's part

Arab," whispered Mel, thinking of Ankar. "That's why he's so fine." But Mel would have given anything if it had been Buttons there in the stall, no matter how pretty James was.

They had dinner with Mr. Blake. Everywhere horse-show people, derbied, cowboy-hatted, bare-headed, bald, fat, thin, were talking and laughing and eating dinner. All the snatches of conversation, all the jokes and whispers, all were horse-talk. Some of it Mel could not even understand. "They all look so, well, so professional," whispered Mel, gazing at the proper riding coats in tweed and plaid, the English riding suits, matching coats and jodhpurs, expensive and new-looking, at the frontier pants and fancy Western boots. Even the Levi's and Western straw hats looked glamorous. "I don't think I'm very hungry," said Mel, feeling small and shabby and very, very unprofessional.

"She's having stage fright," said Mr. Blake later. "She'll be all right tomorrow."

"Yes," said Mother, "she'll be all right tomorrow."

"Yes," said Aunt Kelly, grinning.

Up early, the sun just showing, Mel was all right. There was too much happening to be otherwise. She ate pancakes and bacon with stableboys and grooms and riders and owners, elbow to elbow, stable dogs sneaking in for handouts, people coming and going on errands, with messages, calling back and forth between the tables, leaving suddenly when summoned. Everywhere there was the tense stir of anticipation, of eager, concentrated activity. One lady in jodhpurs and sweater was crying at the table, others comforting her. "What happened?" Mel asked Zee Zee.

"Her horse came up lame," said Zee Zee. "I heard her say so." And above the smell of pancakes and bacon and eggs and coffee was the smell of hay and leather, and especially the clean, healthy smell of properly cared for horses.

"Will we school Rambler this morning?" Mel asked Mr. Blake.

"No, we'll let him rest. James, too. Come help me braid this mare up, then you can look around. Your classes are not until this afternoon." As if she had to be told! Mel held the wet sponge for Mr. Blake and handed him the yarn as he braided.

"There are breeding classes this morning," said Aunt Kelly when Mel had finished. "Come on, hurry." The breeding classes were half over when they got to the stands.

They had passes to the exhibitors' section, where they sat on folding wooden chairs. All around there were booted legs propped on the rail, horse-talk, stable dogs sitting with their masters or sleeping under their feet.

There were classes for each breed, divided into stallions and mares. The judges motioned the horses to move out one by one, led smartly by their grooms, then to line up again to be looked over, point by point. The girls each picked their own choice. Sometimes they were right, more often, wrong. The people around them were doing the same thing—the only difference was that they were usually right.

Outside the ring there were horses schooling; the girls could see them from where they sat. There were hunters practicing over fences, the riders in Levi's and sweaters; and there were stock horses working on gunny sacks, backing to keep the ropes taut and watching the straw-stuffed sacks just as if they were calves. One jumper was being worked back and forth over a fence where two men stood, one at either side, jerking the bar up to hit the horse's legs each time he went over.

"But that's cruel," said Zee Zee, indignant.

"No, it's not," said Mel. "It's only to make him tuck up his feet. Watch." This time the horse jumped high and clear, tucking up nicely. The men did not throw the pole. The rider patted the horse on the neck, the trainer came up and rubbed his ears, and he was led away to be cooled. "See?" said Mel.

"Yes," said Zee Zee, "but I still think it must hurt him."

"Pooh," said Mel.

"What's the Get-of-sire?" asked Zee Zee, looking at her program.

"I think it's judging the colts of one stallion," said Mel, "to see how good he is."

"Oh, look," cried Zee Zee, "just look!"

A black Saddlebred stallion, mane flowing, tail high and full, like a plume, was being led into the ring. Behind him came three mares, each with a colt, and behind them, three grown horses, all black, all as beautiful as their sire. In the stands the sound of talking hushed and changed, becoming a pleased murmur. Several people hurried into the stands and sat down to watch, and people began to gather at the gate and along the fence. Even some of those schooling horses sent the horses to the barns and came to lean on the rail to watch this favorite class. One of the colts bucked and flapped his curly tail.

Behind the Saddlebreds came an Arab stallion, neck bowed, mincing, golden-chestnut coat shining like the sun. He had two grown horses behind him, one a stallion, and two mares with young colts. "Ankar is prettier," whispered Zee Zee. "I wish he were here." She could just see Ankar, shining and prancing, the three mares behind him, the three colts playing and kicking. "I wish Will could have come."

"Shh," said Mel. "Someone will hear you. But so do I. He would have won, I know he would."

The third stallion was coming through the gate. He had only two yearlings and one small colt with its mother. "I think he's a Standardbred," said Mel. "I'm not sure."

The gatekeeper was closing the gate. "That's all," he called to the ringmaster; then, looking around, he opened the gate again just as the judge, looking at his list, questioned, "One more?" They could hear the trotting, and into the ring, neck bowed, came the last entry.

"It looks like Ankar," squealed Zee Zee, sitting straight up in her chair.

"Not as pretty," said Mel loyally.

"It's Will," shrieked Zee Zee, grabbing Mel by the shoulders. "Mel, it is, it's Will."

It was Will. Through the gate behind him came Shelastra, Tickalong, and the Night Princess, each with her colt, one bucking.

"It's Will, it's Will." Both girls were jumping up and down in their chairs.

"Shh," said Mother and Aunt Kelly together. "Shh, people are staring."

"There's Mr. Blake," said Mel, a little quieter but not much.

"Shh," said Mother again.

"But how can it be Will?" whispered Zee Zee. "Why didn't he tell us?" She was twisting the program into a knot. Aunt Kelly took it from her and patted her hand.

"Be still and watch the class. You're distracting Will." It was true, Will was looking up into the stands at them, anxious. Ankar was snorting and pawing.

"Be still, Zee Zee," whispered Mel.

"Yes," said Zee Zee. They held hands tightly.

The Saddlebred stallion was led out at a trot, the mares and colts following.

"Did you know?" whispered Zee Zee softly, touching Aunt Kelly's arm.

"Yes," said Aunt Kelly. "And so did your Mother."

"But is it safe?" whispered Zee Zee.

"Yes," said Aunt Kelly, "it is."

"But what happened?" asked Mel.

"We'll tell you after," whispered Mother and Aunt Kelly together. Two more horses were coming into the ring, the gate opening for them, closing behind them. They joined Will. The girls looked at Aunt Kelly; Aunt Kelly was grinning. "They are Ankar's," she said. "They were born on the ranch, before the fire." They were nearly as handsome as Ankar. Both were gray, both stallions. There was a mutter from the crowd.

When the first Arab group was led out the crowd mumbled admiringly. Mel and Zee Zee frowned. "Anyone can see that Ankar is better," whispered Zee Zee.

"Shh," said Mother again.

Then Ankar was led forward, neck bowed, feet on air, the mares following, colts snorting, the two stallions blowing and prancing. The crowd did not mutter. There was a little silence. Then someone clapped. Someone else joined, and in a second the whole grandstand, the men at the rail, the people in the exhibitors' section, all were clapping, even whistling shrilly. Ankar snorted and side-stepped, Will putting a hand up to calm him, talking softly to him. He quieted a little. The judges were whispering among themselves, conferring, looking again at the line of horses.

The clapping stopped. There was a great waiting hush.

"They can't choose anyone else," said Zee Zee indignantly.

"Maybe they're deciding on second," said Mel, wiser.

"Yes," said Zee Zee, "maybe." But her heart was in her mouth, her knees feeling weak. "Please," she whispered under her breath, "oh, please."

Chapter 24

The judges walked out from the center of the ring to the line of horses. One was carrying a blue ribbon and a huge silver trophy. He paused at the Saddlebred, saying something. The crowd rumbled faintly. Then he went on. Then he was handing the trophy to Will. The crowd cheered and Ankar snorted and pawed.

Zee Zee was crying. So was Mel. They knocked their chairs over to get out of the stand and down to the gate, Aunt Kelly and Mother right behind them.

The last colt was just leaving the ring when they got there. Will stood to one side, holding Ankar and talking to Mr. Blake. Both girls grabbed him, spooking Ankar, who pulled back a little, snorting. Nobody said a thing; they all laughed giddily, the girls fingered the trophy, and

Mr. Blake and Mother and Aunt Kelly grinned broadly. Will blushed, then looked pale.

"Let's get these horses back to the barn," said Mr. Blake. "We're blocking the road. Then we'd better have lunch. You have the first class, Mel."

"I don't think I'm hungry again," said Mel, smelling the frying hamburgers.

"All right," said Mr. Blake, ordering a hamburger for her anyway, "if you don't want it, don't eat it."

Aunt Kelly was telling the whole story, Will sitting solemn and quiet. "How stupid I was," said Will finally, "not to have asked more questions, not to have stayed to find out. I might have known Mr. Stebens would make another record of it."

"Not at all," said Aunt Kelly. "The attorney should have known the day he came to you, but he didn't. Naturally, that frightened you."

"Why didn't he?" asked Zee Zee.

"It was in a codicil," said Aunt Kelly, "an addition to the will. It was in a safe-deposit box, not found till later. By that time Will was gone, and so was Johnny. Will was too well hidden. The lawyers were looking for him but couldn't find a trace."

"But how did you ever know, Aunt Kelly?" Mel asked. "How did you know they were looking?"

Aunt Kelly smiled, her eyes crinkling. "When I told your mother that you had brought Will to see me, she had already found out the names of the lawyers. We made some phone calls, discreetly at first, knowing it might hurt Will. When it looked as if we were on the right track, I went to see the attorneys. Then of course the whole thing came out, and I told Will."

"But what now?" asked Zee Zee. "You won't stay in the cave? Where will you go, Will? What will you do?"

"I won't go far," said Will, grinning.

"No," said Aunt Kelly, "not far."

"To Mr. Blake's?" cried Mel and Zee Zee together. Will nodded.

Their hamburgers were being served. Mel wolfed hers. It was gone before she knew it. "I'm still nervous," said Mel later. "I just forgot for a minute."

"Get dressed," said Mother, pulling the blue curtain of the tack room. "Wash your face in this bucket and comb your hair. Wash your neck, too. There now. Clean shirt, clean socks." The jodhpurs felt delightfully snug and professional, the boots shone.

Will tied her tie for her. "Were you nervous?" whispered Mel.

"Just for Ankar. I wanted him to win," said Will, dark eyes intense.

"Yes," said Mel, patting Rambler's neck. "They aren't nervous, are they?"

"Not Rambler," said Will. "Ankar has never been in a show ring before."

Rambler wasn't nervous. He liked the show ring. He was steady and smart as a whip. "He likes the crowd," said Mr.

Blake. It was true, he did. Out of the corner of his eye Rambler was watching the grandstand. Everything he did was animated, everything perfect.

"Remember," said Mr. Blake, "this is English Pleasure Horses. How you do doesn't count, it's Rambler, but you must make him do his best. Stay away from the rail, don't get clogged up in a bunch of horses, keep him out where the judges can see him."

It was a big class; there were a great many horses, most ridden by grownups. There were three-gaited saddle horses, and several hunters and jumpers, the hunters braided like Rambler. There were plain pleasure horses and one polo pony who was too high and unsettled for the class.

In they went, one at a time, each rider as well-groomed as his horse, each with a number on his back. Mel's face was white and tense, her knuckles pale from gripping the reins so hard, her feet feeling like stones.

She was giving herself directions: *Keep away from the other horses, make him walk, don't let him break. Make him trot out nice and animated, reverse to the center of the ring. Canter slow as he will go, be sure about his lead, turn out, so, then back, then into a canter. The judge is watching. Can he canter slower? Don't let him break. Reverse again, easy now, and trot.* Oh, darn! A bunch of horses were moving around her, crowding her.

Either slow down or speed up, trot him out faster, easy, easy, he almost broke, in toward the center now, there. She cut Rambler over behind one of the three-gaited horses, its high bare tail crooked, she remembered later.

Look out! Jerking sideways, ears back, the horse was going to kick. Rambler shied to the side. *Hold him steady, get him over, don't let him break!*

Whack, a shower of dirt in her face, but they were clear. She couldn't see. *Hold him steady, steady.* Rambler never broke once. *There, a nice clear space, the ringmaster is calling a walk. Pull him up easy, so.* Mel's eyes stung terribly.

"Line up," the ringmaster called.

Easy, easy. The three-gaited horse was lining up next to her. Mel didn't see the judge frowning, but Rambler saw the horse put back his ears. Rambler moved aside a little. The judge walked to the rider and asked him to move down the line, by himself.

"He's out of the money," said Mr. Blake from the gate. "And the judges are sure looking at Mel. What's the matter with her?" In the stands Zee Zee and Mother and Aunt Kelly and Will were on the edge of their chairs, breathless.

Mel, reins in one hand, was trying, with a handkerchief, to get the tanbark out of her eyes. It stung terribly; her eyes were watering so badly that she could not see the other four horses move out at the judges' direction. She didn't see the judge call her, too, even the second time.

The judge stepped toward her. "What's the matter?" he asked; then he could see. He called the ring steward over, and went on down the line.

"Here, lean over," said the steward, taking his own handkerchief from his pocket. "Open your eyes." It hurt like fire. "Now, there, how is that?" asked the steward. It was much better; Mel smiled waterily. "Now get out there," said the steward. "Can you see?" Mel nodded.

The horses were at a trot. Mel joined them, keeping to herself. Canter again, reverse. Dismount and mount. No small job for Mel on the big stallion. Then line up once more.

"It wasn't me," said Mel afterward. "It was Rambler, he was wonderful."

"It was both of you," said Mr. Blake, hanging Mel's blue ribbon on the door, right at the top. "You handled yourself very well. How're your eyes?"

"Much better," said Mel.

"You'll need them soon," said Mr. Blake. "Think you'll be all right?"

"Yes," said Mel, pink with victory, "I'll be all right."

"Lie down and rest," said Mr. Blake. "I'll call you."

"I'm not tired," said Mel.

"You rest," said Mr. Blake. Mel did.

"Children's Hunters next," said Mr. Blake to Mother. "I wish it were tomorrow, to give her more time in the ring."

"How will she do? Will she be all right?" asked Mother.

"She'll do fine," said Mr. Blake. "But more time in the ring would help her. She's doing very well for a green rider. She won't get hurt on Rambler," he added, seeing Mother's face.

Chapter 25

Carrying peanut butter, jelly, and bread, the small boys descended to the basement, sprawling on boxes, drinking milk from the carton.

"You stupid idiot," said Spencer, "it was my sister."

"My gosh, what was she doing there?" whispered another boy.

"What difference does it make?" said Spence, spreading peanut butter and staring balefully at the pile of boxes where the gun still protruded, partially hidden. "The police are after us, what difference does it make what she was doing there?"

"Yeah, you shouldn't have shot his sister," said another boy, giggling.

"Shut up," said Spence.

"I didn't shoot his sister," said the first boy. "I only shot her old horse. I didn't hurt him, anyway."

"How do you know?" asked another. "Maybe the police said that to trap us."

"Aw, shut up," said Spence again. "He's not hurt. I heard them say so."

"Shot a horse," said another with a giggle. "Think your snake can eat a horse? Whatdya think you've got, a boa constrictor?"

"Shut up," said Spence for the third time. "We've got to figure what to do with this gun." He wished he had never seen it.

"Leave it right where it is," the other boys chorused.

"Leave it where it is, Spence," the biggest one said.

"Yeah, Spence," said another, "or we'll tell."

"What're you going to tell," said Spence, "without telling about yourselves?"

"You'll find out."

"Well, you can't leave it here," said Spence, "because if you do I'll call the police myself."

"You do, and we'll say you did it," they told him. "We wiped the fingerprints off."

"All right," said Spence, defeated. "Cover it up and get out of here. It's nearly dinnertime."

Mel was looking at the diagrams of jumps posted on the board by the show office. Mr. Blake was standing beside her and Zee Zee was eating a hot dog. "I'm not hungry," said Mel. This time she meant it. "I'm glad it's not the Handy Class," she said. "I could never remember all that."

The diagram for Handy Hunters looked like a puzzle diabolically contrived. Mel followed the arrows. "My gosh," she said.

"Pay attention to your own class," said Mr. Blake. "Look here. When you come into the ring you canter in a small circle once, to your right. It is a perfectly simple course, four jumps—one, two, three, four—twice around. Don't forget that. And don't pause when you come to the gate. It's way-of-going that counts, smooth and easy, cantering on, but smooth and easy. Don't let him chop."

"Yes, sir," said Mel, wondering if she was going to be nervous again as she went into the ring. She felt sure she was.

And, of course, she was. Worse than before. "Where is Will?" Mel whispered to Mr. Blake as he led her toward the ring.

"He's saddling Ankar," said Mr. Blake. "We put him in the hackamore class. It's next."

"Oh, my," said Mel, forgetting herself for a minute, her eyes getting bigger.

"Think about that later," said Mr. Blake. "Not now. Think about what you're doing, Mel."

"Yes, sir," said Mel, trying not to think about it so much she turned to jelly.

"Watch the first go," said Mr. Blake as they stood at the gate. Mel was sixth in line.

The first horse was a Thoroughbred mare, smaller than Rambler. The child was very small, pink-coated, a boy much younger than Mel, wearing a black hunting cap. His horse was braided with red. If he can do it, so can I, thought Mel, jealous of the way he looked. I'm bigger.

Knowing what she was thinking, Mr. Blake touched her arm. "You watch that boy, he'll give his horse a good ride," said Mr. Blake.

He did. A real professional ride. Even Mel could tell that. There was a great deal of applause from the stands.

The next two children were larger, competent-looking girls. Then there was a girl Mel's age on what appeared to be a rent horse. She did poorly, the horse sticky and lazy over the jumps, pulling at the bit in between.

Then there was a tiny little girl—"No more than a baby," said Aunt Kelly—mounted on a Hackney pony, neat and braided in pale blue. The jumps were not high, but for the pony they were something. The crowd was very quiet, hushed, so as not to disturb the pony. After the last jump they roared, clapping, cheering. The little girl left the ring, serious and steady, but with a slight blush rising to her cheeks at the applause. Mel saw her hug her pony as she dismounted.

Then it was Mel's turn. She no longer felt frightened; she felt disappointed, outclassed. But not Rambler, she thought. He's not outclassed, anyway.

Mr. Blake patted her knee, patted Rambler's neck, and sent them into the ring. For Rambler, thought Mel, I must make him win.

Circle once, she told herself. *Put him in the right lead, gently, straightaway to the first jump, head him into the center, now, reach for his ears, so, and they were over and heading for the second jump. Steady, steady, not too fast,*

don't let him look at the crowd. She pulled him and spoke sharply.

The third jump was a hedge, the fourth a black-and-white road gate; then the brick wall again, the rail, Rambler nicely collected between jumps. Why, it's easy, thought Mel, just like at home. She realized a little too late she had not put him into the turn just right; she was not paying attention when Rambler glanced at the crowd. *Look out!* Too late she knew they were into the jump wrong, crooked. Rambler twisted to clear it and Mel lost her stirrup, sprawling over the saddle. *Quick,*

quick, the stirrup! She couldn't find it with her foot. *Get him steady, lined up for the next jump.* The stirrup was flopping, but Rambler went on, steady as a rock now, making a perfect jump over the gate, Mel clinging awkwardly, then straightening up, trying to look composed going out of the gate.

"It was my fault," said Mel, "I let him get off stride."

"That," said Mr. Blake, "is how you learn. Some of these children have been riding since they could walk. Listen now, they're calling the winners."

"They won't call me," said Mel.

"Shhh," said Mr. Blake.

They did call Mel—for fourth. "That's not bad," said Mr. Blake. Mel led Rambler into the ring, trotting, to get their ribbon. She felt very small, going in on foot.

"You haven't anything now until the last class," said Mr. Blake. "Go up in the stands and watch Will. I'll have one of the boys cool out Rambler."

Mother and Aunt Kelly and Zee Zee were already there. Mel felt pink and a little uncomfortable, knowing she had not done her best, but no one mentioned it. Zee Zee had saved her a hot dog.

Ankar was beautiful. Will had him brushed and shining, in his best braided hackamore and a black-and-white saddle blanket; his hoofs were polished with bootblack and Mr. Blake's best black saddle gleamed against his silvery brightness.

Will wore a new white hat, white chaps, and a pale yellow shirt. The girls had never seen him looking so handsome.

There were twelve horses in the class. "That's a big hackamore class," said Mr. Blake, sitting down.

Ankar stood, neck bowed, ears forward, reins loose, watching the other horses, waiting his turn.

It was even better than the night in the park. Ankar turned, dusting Will's boot. He slid farther than any other horse, straight and true, chin tucked under. He figure-eighted and flew backward at just a touch of the reins. He whirled like a dervish, to left and right, Will looking as if he hardly touched the reins.

There was never any question about it. They had the class won from the beginning.

Will was all smiles, Ankar snorty. "I think he likes this business," said Will, laughing, but when Zee Zee came up to him, Will suddenly turned away, face pink.

Why, he is shy, thought Zee Zee.

The trophy was a huge silver horse, rearing. "Like the white ghost," said Aunt Kelly. It stood on the card table in the tack room, next to Mel's silver cup and the silver platter for Get-of-sire. And there were checks which went with Will's trophies. "For a bank account," said Aunt Kelly.

"Yes," said Will.

Chapter 26

"I wonder how Mel's doing," said Linda, slicing cold meat. Deb was washing brushes at the sink, sending a flood of black ink down the drain and into the sink, too. "Can't you do that in the bathroom?" scolded Linda.

"Um," said Deb, still scrubbing. "Would they call us, do you think, if she had won anything?"

"I don't think so," said Linda. "Aunt Kelly said not. She said just keep good thoughts for Mel, and especially for Will."

"Hm," said Deb.

"It's his whole life," said Linda.

"Yes," said Deb, drying. "But I do hope Mel wins something, too. Where is Spence?"

"I don't know," said Linda, setting the table. "He is late. He just doesn't hear, sometimes."

"Mmm," said Debra again. "Shall I go look?"

"Yes," said Linda. "I'll stir this."

Deb did look, everywhere she could think of. She went into the little valley in the park, and even walked the beach. She was gone a good hour, and of course when she got home, there was Spencer eating his dinner, ravenous and dirty. "Why didn't you make him wash?" Deb asked Linda. "Spencer, honestly, how can you get so dirty? And scratched! What have you been doing?" He smelled strange, too. Sticky sweet, thought Deb.

"Nothing," said Spence, mouth full. His face was streaked and muddy.

Behind him Linda shook her head, frowning. "Let him be," she said later to Deb. "Something has happened. He'll tell us quicker if we don't force him."

"What could it be? What has he done now?" said Deb.

"I don't know, but he was almost crying when he came in. I didn't think he'd eat."

"He can always eat," said Deb.

"Why don't you go to the park and play?" said Deb the next morning. All six little boys had converged in Spencer's room, making noise. It bothered Deb. "I can't work with so much yelling," she said.

"We don't want to go to the park," said Spence. "We want to play here. We're feeding our snakes."

"Then be quiet," said Deb. It was true, she couldn't work well with all that hubbub. She shut the studio door. Spencer had not said a word about the night before. I wonder, thought Deb, if I should ask. Spencer hardly ever kept anything to himself for long.

Deb was finishing the last drawings. "How can you be so patient?" asked Linda, bringing her tea. It was exacting work.

"I like it," said Deb. "When the house is quiet, that is."

"Yes," said Linda, "what a ruckus. I almost wish he had gone to the horse show."

"And have him worry Mel? No, he's better here," said Deb, dipping her brush and pursing her lips. "Come and look, this is finished, Lin."

"It's beautiful," said Linda. "Let's stand them all up and look."

"Here," said Deb, "where the bear goes up the tree, do you think this should be darker?"

"No," said Linda, "it's just right. It's only twilight, you know."

They got so engrossed in the drawings that they didn't notice the quiet.

"Maybe they've gone to the park," said Deb when they finally did notice.

"Hm, yes," said Linda. "I hope they stay out of trouble."

"I hope they shut the snakes in," said Deb.

"Better get dressed, Mel," said Mr. Blake, going to saddle the pony. The last class was late; it was almost six. The tack room, with its curtains pulled, was quite dark. Mother lit the unshaded light, which threw strange shadows on the walls from the bridles hanging about and the saddles on their racks. Mel had a long purple bruise on the inside of her leg from going over the jump without a stirrup.

"Does it hurt?" asked Mother.

"No," said Mel, lying a little.

"Here, let me see your hat," said Mother, brushing it.

Zee Zee poked her head in, and saw Mel in chaps and Western shirt, white Western hat tilted jauntily. "We're going up and get a seat, Aunt Kelly and I," she said.

Will was already there, saving chairs. He was wearing his old Levi's and Western shirt once more. "I feel better in these," he said shyly.

They watched the horses come into the ring, the lights on now, making the ring like a stage. Sitting straight, reins loose, red hair peeping out under her hat, Mel looked very smart, James sharp and alert.

"She isn't nervous this time," whispered Will. It was true, she wasn't. Riding one-handed as Will did, the other hand in her belt, Mel was making a show of it. She was at home on a smaller horse, there were no jumps to worry her, and she had already made her mistakes for the day. Ring-wise, now, and feeling cocky, Mel was putting James through his paces with hardly any effort at all.

"Good girl," said Will as James stepped carefully over the logs, slid quickly through the gate which Mel had opened from the saddle, and walked the narrow wooden bridge. "Good girl, Mel, you've won the class, that's sure." And she had, hands down she won it, or rather, "James did," as Mel said later.

They made a party of dinner. Other horse people joined them, one a breeder who talked to Will for a long time.

"He wants to buy the colts," said Will later, "and he wants to breed some of his mares."

"All three colts?" asked Zee Zee sadly.

"No," said Will, "I'll keep Rankashan."

"I knew you would," said Zee Zee, grinning.

"Perhaps," said Will, "someday you'll ride him." Lightly said, it was not lightly meant. Zee Zee thought she was blushing and she turned her head away.

"But there's a night show, Mother," Mel wailed after dinner. "Please, I won't be able to sleep if I go to bed now."

"What do you think?" asked Mother, looking at Mr. Blake.

"A couple of classes shouldn't hurt. She can see the Green Hunters, that would be good for her, and the first jumping class."

"All right," said Mother. "Then right to bed."

"Can I stay a little longer?" asked Zee Zee when Mel was led away yawning.

"Yes," said Mother, "but you're to come when Will does."

"Yes," said Zee Zee, "I promise."

Will walked her to the motel through the dark parts of the show grounds, away from the ring activity, the last-class bustle. "You will work for Mr. Blake, then?" asked Zee Zee.

"Yes," said Will, "it's all arranged."

"But when did you know?" asked Zee Zee. "When did you first know there was proof?"

Will laughed. "I knew when you came to say good-by.

It was hard to keep from laughing, thinking how surprised you'd be. I knew before, but it wasn't until that afternoon that Aunt Kelly was sure. She made all the arrangements about the show, and she paid the entry fees herself. I will pay her back."

They sat for a minute on the fairgrounds fence before they crossed the street to the motel. "I can go back to school, now," said Will, "part time. Aunt Kelly has arranged that, too. She is quite something, Aunt Kelly."

"Yes," said Zee Zee, laughing, "she is. Imagine, her knowing about the ghost all that time, and never telling anyone."

"But you didn't tell, either," said Will.

"But she's a grownup," said Zee Zee.

"I'll watch you to your door from here," said Will, pausing at the edge of the motel yard.

"But aren't you staying at the motel?" asked Zee Zee, surprised.

"No," said Will, "I sleep in Ankar's stall."

"He doesn't mind?" asked Zee Zee.

"No," said Will, "he likes the company."

"But isn't it cold?" asked Zee Zee.

"I have my bedroll," said Will. "I'm used to sleeping out, remember?"

"Yes," said Zee Zee, remembering the cave. Will had no tack room, no colors. Only a tack trunk by Ankar's stall. "You should have colors," said Zee Zee, "colors of your own, Will. Now you'll be showing Ankar. You *will* be showing him?"

"Oh, yes," said Will, "he deserves to be shown. And

there's the money, too." He was thinking of the fat checks Ankar had won and the promised stud fees. "You choose the colors, Zee," said Will. "Next show, we'll have a tack room to put them on."

"Good night," said Zee Zee. "You'll have breakfast with us?"

"If you're early enough," said Will. "Good night."

"What do you want to go up there for?" Spence said with a growl. "That's my sister's room."

"Ya, whata we want to go messing around in a girl's room for?" harped another.

"She the one we shot her horse?" asked the biggest boy.

"Naw," said Spence, "the other one."

"How many ya got, for gosh sake?" asked one.

"Four," said Spencer. "One adopted."

"Haw," said one. "Four sisters. Bet you play with dollies and have tea parties!"

"Shut up," said Spencer.

"Do what?" said the bigger boy, Robby.

"Shut up," said Spence again.

"Don't get so smart," said the boy, "or we'll tell about the gun."

"You'd better not," yelled Spence.

"Hey, what's this?" cried a littler boy, distracting them. "A dollhouse?"

They were standing in Zee Zee's attic, uninvited. Spencer was getting an uneasy feeling in the pit of his stomach.

"C'mon," he said, "let's go."

"Go where?"

"Out," said Spence. "Come on."

"Ya, a dollhouse," said Robby. My sister had one of these. Know what I did to it?"

"No, what?" said two of them, bellying up to the table.

"Ya, I smashed it like this," yelled Robby, raising his fist and crashing it down through the little glass roof.

There was a moment of silence, like a small pearl, then, "We better go," said one of the boys. Spencer stood staring at the house.

"And then . . ." began the boy, raising his hand again.

But he did not finish. Spencer had him by the collar, pounding his ear with his fist, kneeing him in the stomach. They crashed against the table, shaking the little house. "Ya, ya," yelled one of the boys, "ya, fight!" But the others were wiser.

"Come on," said one.

"Yeah," said another, and down the ladder they pelted, all but Spencer and Robby, whose stomach Spence sat on, pounding his face.

A hand grabbed Spencer by the ear, jerking him up. Another hand grabbed Robby, who had leaped for the door. "I didn't know girls could be so strong," said the boy afterward.

Deb and Linda looked at each other, at the boys, and at the little house. "Spencer, how could you!" cried Deb angrily.

"Tell us what happened," said Linda.

It was at that moment that Aunt Vivian's face appeared below. Oh, oh, thought Deb, now it *will* be trouble. But Linda was thinking she was glad for a grownup just then.

The other boys had fled, leaving the front door open.
Aunt Vivian, seeing it so, had come in to investigate. Now
Deb and Linda stood over the two small boys, making
them talk.

Aunt Vivian looked at the house, its roof smashed in,
two walls broken. Then she looked at the boys: Robby,
red-faced and defiant, Spencer angry. "Did you do that?"
demanded Aunt Vivian, looking at Robby.

"Yes," he said, shutting his mouth tight afterward. That
was all he would say, nothing more. His eye was turning
black, and his cheek was bruised. His father was called
to come for him, and Spencer sent to his room.

"You can stay there until Mother gets home," said Deb, "except for meals."

"What about the garden house?" said Linda, worried. "We must try to fix it before Zee Zee sees."

"I will tend to the house," said Aunt Vivian in her imperious way. It sounded strangely comforting and welcome to the girls.

Counting on her fingers, Mel was almost asleep before she had finished. Saturday, English Pleasure Horses, Children's Hunters, Children's Western Trail Horse. For Will, Get-of-sire and Hackamore. Also, Arab Stallions, she thought, remembering. Will had won that class before they had got to the stands.

"It was all planned," Aunt Kelly had said. "We wanted you to see him first in the Get-of-sire."

"Then you kept me to help braid all because of Will?" Mel had asked.

"That's right," Mr. Blake had said. "We had it all timed, and very well, I think," he had added, winking at Aunt Kelly.

So, continued Mel to herself, five firsts, three of them Will's. And a fourth. Why, Ankar has won every class. Maybe he's a magic horse after all, a ghost in horse's lining, thought Mel sleepily, smiling.

Then, tomorrow, she went on, in the morning, Stock Horse eliminations for Will, then, first afternoon class, Ladies' Western Pleasure Horses. Then, Children's Equitation, English first, then Western. Then the Stock Horse for Will. He'll win again, thought Mel. I know he will.

Then, Sunday night, thought Mel, thrilling, the Ladies' Hunters. Third class, Sunday night. Under the ring lights. When she closed her eyes she could see the lighted ring. Will the lights throw shadows under the jumps? she wondered. And frighten Rambler? She was scaring herself. Could she do it? Can I? Can I? wondered Mel. The jumps would be higher, the riders all grownups, or nearly all. She remembered the two girls in the afternoon class. Would they ride in the Ladies'? She remembered with embarrassment her lost stirrup. She hugged her pillow, thinking, I don't have to ride. Mr. Blake can get another rider. Then she saw the lighted ring again, looking like a stage, the brush jump, the black-and-white gate. Well, thought Mel sleepily, it's not till Sunday night, and she was sound asleep, smiling.

Chapter 27

Aunt Vivian was repairing the little house. "You can stay
overnight if you like," Deb offered. "It's certainly nice of
you to help."

"All right," said Aunt Vivian, "I will. I must admit I'm
enjoying this. I'd forgotten what a pleasure it is to build
something."

"Her face looks softer," said Deb to Linda later. "I'm
glad she said she'd stay."

"Yes," said Linda. They were to be very glad.

Aunt Vivian was glad, too. Tucked away at the top of
the house, alone and secret, the sun streaming in, Aunt
Vivian was getting acquainted with someone she had forgotten. Her nail polish was chipped, her hair astray and
bobbing, her eyes sparkling, her fingers nimble and quick.

She hummed a little tune. Aunt Vivian didn't know it, but she looked very pretty. Very pretty, indeed.

"And you're not to have Jeffy in your room, either," said Deb to Spencer, frowning. "You're to stay in it alone."

"I'm not alone," said Spence. "I have my snakes."

"You're alone," said Deb cruelly.

Linda made Aunt Vivian a special breakfast with strawberry muffins and Canadian bacon and scrambled eggs with cheese.

Aunt Vivian was setting the table. "Where's Spencer this morning?" she asked.

"In his room," said Deb. "He can come down for some cereal when we're finished."

"Mmmm," said Aunt Vivian, not commenting.

"Were the little trees damaged?" asked Linda, pouring milk.

"No," said Aunt Vivian, "only one cracked pot, and I have mended that."

Panda was licking fish from his plate. Aunt Vivian did not even frown at him.

"I do believe she's different," Deb said to Linda later.

"Yes," said Linda, "so do I."

Jeffy sauntered into the kitchen, looking interested in breakfast. He sniffed the cat's dish, getting a cuff on the nose for it, then looked longingly at Linda. "All right," said Linda, "in just one minute." Jeffy drew closer to watch her frying bacon. Then he turned, eyeing the back door. A moment later he was barking frantically, hackles raised, tail down. There was a loud knocking. Jeff sniffed under the door, but did not stop barking.

When Deb opened the door there was a policeman there, uniformed and polished and young. It's about Spencer, she thought. She was right.

"It's nothing much," said the young lieutenant, coming right to the point. "The boys were shooting slingshots. Not a federal offense, but they did get into some mischief —though there's something strange about that."

Linda set a place for the lieutenant and gave him coffee and a muffin. "It was odd," he said, buttering the muffin. "We didn't even know that little shack was there. I thought that cave had been closed up and forgotten long ago."

"A cave?" asked Deb innocently.

"It's a small, hidden valley," said the lieutenant, "almost a cave. It looks as if someone has been keeping horses there, right under our noses." He grinned.

"You mean you found some horses there?" asked Deb, still acting innocent.

"They were gone," said the lieutenant, "but they have been there recently. There were still sacks of feed, broken open by the boys, alfalfa and molasses, and there were some ropes and halters strewn around the shed." He took a third muffin, Linda pouring more coffee.

Molasses, thought Deb, remembering the way Spencer had smelled.

"What would happen to someone who kept horses on park property?" asked Deb, still innocent.

175

Lieutenant Callahan looked closely at her bland face. "A fine," said the young man, "perhaps a short jail sentence."

"A fine, and jail?"

"Perhaps only one or the other." The young man grinned. "Do you know the place I mean?"

"Yes," said Deb, "we do."

"And do you know who has been keeping horses there?"

"Yes, I'm afraid we know that, too." Then she told him the story, all of it. As Will had once said, "Half a story's no good, you might as well tell it all."

They had almost forgotten about Spencer, but finally they came back to him. "The boys wrecked the shed," said Lieutenant Callahan, "first shooting at the roof with slingshots, then climbing down the cliff into the cave and ripping open the door. They tore everything up and made hard balls of the feed, pelting each other. There was a real free-for-all, by the looks of it."

"You didn't catch them at it?" asked Aunt Vivian.

"No," said Lieutenant Callahan. "One of the boys' fathers recognized the smell of alfalfa and molasses, and made his boy take him back there, feeling sure they had destroyed someone's property."

"And they had," said Aunt Vivian.

"But no one there to claim it," said Lieutenant Callahan. "There's also something else. The boy's father says there is a .22 missing. We think it might be the one that was shot in the park. If your Spencer was with the boys, maybe he knows where the gun is."

"You'd better get Spencer," said Aunt Vivian to Deb. "Tell him to come down."

"Your sister's horse was the one shot, wasn't it?" asked the lieutenant.

"The one she rides," said Deb. "He belongs to the stables."

Spence came in, looking frightened. But he did not hedge. "It's in the basement," he said, "but I didn't shoot it. They said they would say I did." He took Lieutenant Callahan to the basement. They came back with the gun.

"I was in the cave, too," said Spence.

"I see," said Lieutenant Callahan.

"What should we do?" asked Aunt Vivian. "I hate to call his mother. It will upset her so, and the girls too." Debra could have hugged her.

"We'll wait until Monday," said Lieutenant Callahan. "She can call the station when she gets home. Spencer says he didn't shoot the gun, and the boy, Will, would have to press charges about the shed. But with it on park property, well, he will have other things to worry about."

"But what about Will?" asked Linda.

"He must come into the station," said the lieutenant. "There will be a bit to clear up about it, a hearing, I'm sure, but from what you tell me about the boy, it should work out all right. Don't worry about it."

"All right," said Aunt Vivian, "we won't." But of course they did. It seemed a very long time until Mother would be home.

"What can we do?" asked Linda.

"Just what the lieutenant said," said Aunt Vivian. "Nothing. We'll work this out together, when your mother gets home."

Sunday morning was dazzlingly bright. There was to be a parade through the fairgrounds. "Will you ride Ankar in it?" Zee Zee asked Will.

"No," said Will, "I want him fresh for the eliminations. But let's go watch the horses get ready."

So they did, all of them, watching the horses saddled, watching the people, some costumed, most in bright colors, with silk Western shirts and fancy chaps—black-and-white cowhide, the fur on, or curly angora—putting the finishing touches to themselves and their horses. Manes were unbraided, combed; hoofs were polished with shoeblack. There were ladies in Spanish dress with lace mantillas riding sidesaddle; mounted guards, troops of them in uniform; hunting teams in red coats and black; horses with saddles so crusted in silver the children wondered how they could carry them.

"Some are all saddle," said Mr. Blake, laughing, "and very little horse underneath."

There were Arabs in Arabian trappings, one ridden by a lady with a sheer, spangled harem skirt, a veil over her face. It was very grand, but, "I like Ankar better in plain things," said Mel.

"So do I," said Will.

"But isn't it fine?" said Aunt Kelly.

It was fine. There were pony teams pulling small buggies, Shetlands pulling a miniature beer wagon, exactly like the monstrous ones hauled by magnificent draft horses. There were gaited horses in harness, and even roadsters harnessed to racing bikes, their drivers dressed in bright silks: yellow and green, red and blue, polka dots.

The children ate cotton candy and hot dogs and popcorn, and for a little while were only fair-goers, nothing more. Then it was time to tend to business again, and Will went to get Ankar ready, Mel and Zee Zee helping him.

When he had ridden off toward the gate, Ankar proud and watchful, Will looking like part of him—"Like he grew in the saddle," said Mel, envious—the rest went to sit in the stands to watch. The eliminations were held in the morning, before the show, to pick only the best for the show itself. "Otherwise," said Mel, "there would be too many." Mr. Blake had told her this. And it was true, the eliminations went on all morning, one horse at a time.

"Why, it could take all afternoon," said Zee Zee.

Ankar was patient, waiting his turn, watching the other horses brightly. The man who had talked to Will at dinner rode up to him on an Arab mare, chestnut like Shelastra, and they sat talking. Mel and Zee could see them from the stands.

Finally, when it was Will's turn, he breezed through, Ankar fresh and beautiful. "Of course," said Mel. "Of course," they all said.

Then it was Mel again, first class after lunch, once more

pale, not hungry. "It's going through the gate," said Mel later. "I'm fine once I'm through, and starving when I come out."

And so she ate candy bars and hamburgers between classes, Mother shaking her head, smiling, and letting her, this once. It was a busy afternoon; Mel, going to the ring, would meet Mr. Blake coming out, and then meet Will going in as she came out. She had Western, then English, then Western again, so that she had to change almost as fast as an actress in a play. Zee Zee found herself holding horses, walking them, trying to see the classes through the rails. Even Aunt Kelly was seen leading James about between classes.

"Well," said Mr. Blake when the afternoon was over and the ribbons were hanging on the door, "that's not so bad, I'd say."

Ankar had won the Stock Horse class. "Of course," said everyone, "what did you expect?" Will blushed.

"He is a magic horse," said Mel.

"Magic or not," said Mr. Blake, "he is the sensation of the show." It was true; more and more people stopped what they were doing to watch Ankar, more and more people came to his stall, some breeders, some buyers, everyone admiring, everyone impressed.

Mother made Mel stand in front of the tack-room door, in front of the row of ribbons, to take her picture. She held her three ribbons for the afternoon, a red for Ladies' Western Pleasure Horses, a white for Western Equitation, and a blue for English. Mel sighed, content. "And now a nap," said Mother, "until dinnertime."

"All right," said Mel without another word.

"She has had a hard day," said Mr. Blake when she had gone. "I'm mighty proud of her."

"And so am I," said Mother. "So am I."

In the motel room Mel napped fitfully. "I get jittery, thinking about it," she said. "They'll all be grown people, or almost all."

"Well, don't get jittery," said Mother. "Do you realize you have beaten professionals today? Do you, Mel?"

"Rambler has," said Mel, "and James. But the Ladies' Hunters, Mother! I don't think I can!"

"You don't have to," said Mother. "You can change your mind."

"Of course I'll ride," said Mel, and promptly went to sleep.

Mother waked her before dinner, in time to dress. Spiffed and polished, fresh and rested, she felt better. She knew she looked right, black coat neat, hair tied back with black ribbon, boots polished. *I feel like I belong,* thought Mel, looking around at the other riders. Will smiled at her, and winked.

Rambler was braided and polished, too. "Ladies' Hunters, Ladies' Hunters," the announcer boomed. Mel was first up for the class. The ring lights shown, figures clustered by the gate, riders waited their turn behind her. "Number seventeen, Rambler," said the speaker, "Miss Melani Heath up," and she was in the ring, circling at a slow canter.

Now pick him up a little, she thought. *Into the first jump, so, don't let him look at the stands.* The jumps were higher this time. The first one loomed at her like a mountain. They were over it, smooth and clean, before she had time to worry, and into the second. Just as nice. Now the turn. She held him steady, keeping his head from the crowd. Into the third, the fourth, around again, clean and pretty as a picture.

"That's in the money," said Mr. Blake, taking Rambler's bridle as he came through the gate. He undid the girth, put up the stirrups, and removed the saddle.

They watched the other horses go, nine of them, one of the girls from the Children's class among them. "There were several good goes," said Mr. Blake when the last horse had left the ring, "but you're in the money all right," and he rubbed the last saddle marks from Rambler's back.

The ringmaster was calling them back to line up. He walked down the line and back, slowly, looking at the stripped horses. Down once more, and back, stopping to look Rambler over. Then he walked to the judges' stand in the center of the ring and gave a slip of paper to the steward, who ran with it to the announcer. A lady in a long white satin dress, wearing orchids, was coming into the ring, escorted by a man in a tuxedo. How grand, thought Mel, forgetting all about herself.

The judge handed the lady the trophy, and stood beside her as the speakers boomed out, announcing the winner: "First place in the Ladies' Hunters, this evening, Ladies and Gentlemen, is Rambler, ridden by Miss Melani Heath," and Mel was going forward in a kind of daze to take the trophy. It was so big she could hardly see over it as she left the ring at a run, leading Rambler at a

fast trot, his head turned, watching the stands applaud him.

Aunt Kelly and Mother and Zee Zee and Will and Mr. Blake were all standing up, shouting and cheering and waving. Rambler bowed his neck and lifted his feet like a saddle horse, switching his tail and bobbing his chin, every inch a ham, nearly knocking Mel down as he looked over his shoulder going through the gate. There everyone greeted her, Will taking the heavy trophy, Mr. Blake giving her a leg up, bareback, to be trotted to the barn in style, waving her ribbon, glowing with excitement.

In front of the tack room there was a great bucket filled with ice, and real champagne glasses on the card table.

While Mel sat on Rambler, still holding her ribbon, Mother handed her the trophy and took a flash picture of her. Then Mr. Blake popped the cork of the champagne, and everyone toasted Mel, Zee Zee and Will having just a little bit. Mel had a tiny glass, too. "It's bitter!" she said. Zee Zee nodded.

Mother took a picture of them all, with their glasses raised. Then Mel walked Rambler out, Zee Zee and Will going with her, through the quieter part of the grounds. They listened to the show sounds in the distance: the announcer's voice faint, the crowd cheering, then silent; the music coming from the ferris wheel and rides on the other side of the fairgrounds. Nobody talked much. Their last class had come and gone, and been won, the last night of the show was drawing to a close. Everyone a little sad, a little sleepy, they just walked along cozily beside Rambler, who was warm and steamy and nice, his horsy breath tickling as he nuzzled Mel's neck.

Chapter 28

They followed the horse van home early the next morning, Mel sleeping contentedly most of the way. She had already done a good morning's work, helping pack the saddles and bridles and blankets neatly away in the tack trunks, the medicines and bottles of leg brace, the curry combs and brushes all in their places. The horses had been blanketed, their legs wrapped, and they were haltered and tied short to their mangers in the van. The colts, too, were tied next to their mothers, Will riding in the van with them to see that they rode well. The van drove slowly, carefully, the car following.

Mother woke Mel as they pulled into the stable yard. "You'll want to help put the horses away," she said.

"Yes," said Mel, foggy.

Will was unloading the first colt. "Where will you put them?" asked Zee Zee.

"Come and see," said Will. There were four nice stalls at the end of the barn, bedded with fresh, sweet straw, and all with big paddocks in back. Over each stall there was a freshly painted sign, the first one saying *Ankar*, with Will's name underneath.

"Why, look," said Zee Zee, pointing; then she called: "Mel, Mel, come and look!"

"There's Buttons," shouted Mel, running up. "They've moved his stall next to Will's!" She ran to say "Hello" to Buttons. The pony nickered softly. "I think he missed me," said Mel, delighted.

"But look at his sign, Mel," said Zee Zee, pulling her back. Mel looked. Buttons's name was painted freshly in gold. But there was more. "I don't understand," said Mel, perplexed. The sign said *Melani Heath*.

"Look here," said Mother, laughing. Below the sign, on the lower door, right in front of her, was a large white card with a photograph on it. It was Buttons's picture, with Mel in her show clothes. HAPPY UN-BIRTHDAY, the sign said; then, under the picture, HAPPY NEW PONY FOR MEL, FOR ALWAYS.

Mel still didn't understand. She read the card three times, mouth open, staring.

"He's your pony now," said Mother. "He belongs to you, Mel."

Linda and Deb had a party ready. Aunt Vivian had baked a cake. "Let's don't spoil it," said Deb. "Let's tell Mother afterward. And Will."

"Yes," said Linda. "If Mel didn't win, it would be too much. And too much for Will, too."

But Mel had won, and Will. The ribbons were brought home, and the trophies, and the checks displayed. Um, thought Deb, those will go to pay the fine. I hope it isn't more than that.

It was a very fine party. No one spoiled it, not even Spence, who was as good as gold, though quiet. "Are you all right?" asked Mother, feeling his cheek. He said he was.

Late that afternoon Mel rode Buttons to the park—out into the valley where he had gotten away from Zee Zee, and then, softly, through the grass under the willow tree where he had hidden from her. He wanted to graze. She let him, bridle and all. "You won't run off again, now you're mine forever, will you?" whispered Mel. Buttons cocked an ear. "Will you?" Mel repeated. Buttons didn't answer. Mel hugged him.

That same afternoon Mother went to see Lieutenant Callahan. Will went with her, grim-faced.

And in the big old house, quiet and sunny, Aunt Vivian went up to Zee Zee's attic.

"But you mended it just fine," said Zee Zee. "I would never have known. It was awfully nice of you."

"Well," said Aunt Vivian, laughing, "I guess this house started something. I don't know when I have enjoyed myself so much. Not since I was a girl. I have a spot at home, by a window, where I have put a big table. You'd be surprised how many scraps of wood and things one can beg from shops and carpenters and seamstresses and such."

Zee Zee smiled. Aunt Vivian continued, "The first house I am going to build will be like this," and she took a pencil and a piece of paper and began to draw the plan. "I think," said Aunt Vivian, "that it will be a summer house, away in the mountains. It will be one big room, with cupboards for sleeping, like the Dutch have, and here..." Before Zee Zee and Aunt Vivian knew it the light was growing dim, and Linda was calling dinner. Houses danced in Zee Zee's mind, and Aunt Vivian's, houses with Spanish courts and balconies, houses on the sides of steep hills, many-storied; houses with terrace roofs that could be pulled down in winter to shut them up like turtles; all manner of houses, growing as they planned them.

"The next one," said Zee Zee, "the next one..." And down they went to dinner.

A fire was blazing and they could smell chicken roasting. Mel, dirty and happy, was curled before the fire. Will, very scrubbed, and Mr. Blake smiled in the doorway and then settled themselves, too, by the fire. Spencer looked brighter, Mother content. Aunt Kelly, cross-legged on the hearth, was sipping sherry and feeding Jeffy crackers. Panda lay curled in the best yellow chair, near the window. Aunt Vivian sat on the couch next to Linda, taking the sherry Lin offered her.

"I think," said Mr. Blake, "that this has been a very fine summer."

They all agreed that it had.

"And a wonderful weekend," said Mother, "every bit of it. My, that Lieutenant Callahan has such a nice smile." Deb was blushing, but only Zee Zee saw her. Spencer smiled, relieved. Will, too.

"School is starting soon," said Mother. "Will will go with you, Zee, until he catches up."

"Perhaps," said Mr. Blake, "Will could use some help at first. It's been awhile since he's had time for lessons."

"Yes," said Will, "I think I could, if Zee Zee doesn't mind."

"I don't mind," said Zee Zee, wondering if she, too, were going to blush, but she did not. Perhaps, thought Zee Zee, school will not be so bad, after all.

"And Mr. Blake says," Mel announced, "that I can work for Buttons's keep on weekends. I'm to help the beginners! And I'm to exercise James!"

"A very fine summer, indeed," said Aunt Vivian, smiling, "for every one of us. Now I know what tending your business does mean! And Deb and I have a surprise, too." Aunt Vivian looked at Linda. "We have taped Linda's book. After dinner, perhaps we can play it, if Linda doesn't mind."

"Oh," said Linda. "My! I don't know!"

"It sounds wonderful," said Deb. "Won't you share it, Lin?"

"Oh, my," said Linda again. "Well, of course I will!"

"And we'll have the drawings out," said Mother. "I think they are just right." Deb beamed.

"A very fine summer, indeed," said Aunt Kelly, giving Jeffy another cracker. "A very fine summer indeed."

"Then we won't see the white ghost in the fog anymore?" Mother was saying to Will. They were standing on the porch, bidding Will and Mr. Blake good night.

"Perhaps you'll see him," Will said, smiling shyly. "I can still ride in the park. Unless the judge decides against it." He grinned. "Ankar will still like to go there. I used to sit on the hill while he grazed and look out over the mists. It always seemed as if he could see so far; as if he could see his future. And maybe he could—maybe he could."

"Do you think she really likes it?" Linda whispered to Deb in the kitchen.

"Aunt Kelly?" asked Deb. "Of course she does. She wouldn't lie. And so does everyone. Tomorrow we'll mail it, Lin."

"Good night," said Linda.

"Good night, Lin," said Deb.

But long after they had said good night Deb could hear the woodpecker-tapping of Linda's typewriter. A new book, a new book, thought Deb sleepily. I wonder what it will be. . . .

And upstairs a little girl looked out of her window, sitting up in bed. He's mine, he's my pony, thought Mel. She could hardly believe it; though in a way it seemed as if he had always been hers, or they each other's.

I wonder, Did I give him enough hay? thought Mel. Did I fill his water bucket? I wonder, Can he open his door? Oh, dear! But then she breathed a sigh of relief. Will had fixed it for her.

Jeffy was curled up on her bed, taking most of the foot, snoring a little. He and Panda were glad to have their bedmates back; it had been lonesome without them.

Panda was not in bed yet, but curled on top of Zee Zee's desk, having his stomach rubbed, for Zee Zee was not sleepy. She sat petting Panda and watching the ocean.

There was phosphorescence on the waves, making them luminous. The sand was white in the moonlight. I wonder, thought Zee Zee, where it will take us—the moon and the sea and this house. I wonder where time will take us; we're growing up. It's so nice like it is. I wonder if we have to get older. Then, later, she thought: I wonder what I'll do when I do get older. I wonder, Could I build a real house like the small one? I wonder, Would I want to? Would I?

Then she squeezed Panda tight, for below her on the beach, stepping lightly in the lace-edged surf, was the white ghost. This time he had a rider. He's looking up, thought Zee Zee. He's looking up at my window. I wonder if he can see me. No, of course not. The room was quite dark behind her. Will sat a long time, Ankar pawing lightly at the lapping water; then they turned and galloped off along the beach, out of sight.

Zee Zee sat still a little longer, then crawled snug into bed, Panda close to warm her. If I want to build houses, she thought, then, that's what I shall do. The moon peeped in at her, the surf lapped faintly, and Panda purred beside her ear. If a boy can hide a ghost, thought Zee Zee, smiling, and all the little ghosts, then I guess a girl can build houses. "I guess she can, hmmm, Panda?" Perhaps Panda thought she could, but he didn't say a thing; he only purred.